Glass shattered as the bomb crashed through the window

"Grenade!" Bolan yelled as the dark spherical object sailed into the room. "Hit the floor!"

The Executioner dived off the chair, landing hard, rolling. He heard the thump of Sloan's feet, realizing in that instant that the DEA agent had gone off the bed on the same side as the grenade.

"Ed..." he called.

The rest of his words were lost as the grenade detonated. The blast hammered at Bolan's senses. He felt the floor shudder, and it seemed as if the whole room were moving. Debris rained on him, glass exploded, objects crashed against the walls.

Bolan had the Beretta in hand when he eventually got to his feet, his ears ringing. He stared through the haze of smoke that lay like a gauzy curtain across his vision. He looked at the window.

His mind clicked back into gear. An attack at this point in the mission meant that he'd been made. Either Ed Sloan had slack security, or someone in the police department was dirty.

MACK BOLAN®
The Executioner

DON PENDLETON'S
THE EXECUTIONER®
FEATURING MACK BOLAN®

SUDDEN FURY

A GOLD EAGLE BOOK FROM
WORLDWIDE®

TORONTO • NEW YORK • LONDON
AMSTERDAM • PARIS • SYDNEY • HAMBURG
STOCKHOLM • ATHENS • TOKYO • MILAN
MADRID • WARSAW • BUDAPEST • AUCKLAND

First edition May 1994.

ISBN 0-373-61185-4

Special thanks and acknowledgment to
Michael Linaker for his contribution to this work.

SUDDEN FURY

Printed in U.S.A.

The success of a war is gauged by the amount of damage it does.

—Victor Hugo

Colombian drug lords operate on a single minded philosophy. They choose their area of operation, move in and set up shop regardless of social or moral considerations. Anyone who stands in their way is wiped out. In order to survive, the War on Drugs *must* continue.

—Mack Bolan

PROLOGUE

Kingston, Jamaica

Winston Rogers realized he'd been tagged the morning he spotted three of Royal Doucette's heavies watching his apartment.

Doucette was running interference and local business for the Colombians in Kingston. He was a local hood using the cartel to elevate his status in the community. Tying in with the drug traffickers and helping them become established on the island had improved Doucette's financial standing, as well. Previous to their arrival he had managed to make a halfway decent living from crime—protection, prostitution, a little drug business. The Colombians, in the shape of Rio Santos and his organization, had filled the Jamaican with hope for the future. He accepted the cartel's offer without hesitation, becoming a willing pawn in their Caribbean venture.

The growing threat that the cartel posed in the Caribbean area had come to the notice of the American DEA. They saw the Colombians using Jamaica as yet another staging post for the import of drugs to the

U.S. mainland. An undercover DEA agent was planted on the island, with the cooperation of the Jamaican government. They didn't want the island's reputation tainted by the establishment of a thriving drug trade. The DEA agent was provided with local help in the form of a female police officer. She brought in Winston Rogers, who had worked with the Kingston PD for a number of years as a civilian undercover agent.

Working from the thinnest possible brief, the trio began to build its case against the cartel. Progress was slow, the investigation hampered at the outset by the lack of information. The fear of exposure meant that every move the three made had to be done under the strictest care. Gathering hard evidence that would stand up in court was both time-consuming and exhausting.

The investigation began to show promise. Piece by piece the evidence grew, each fragment helping to form the overall picture.

And then Ed Sloan, the DEA agent, came up with something none of them had anticipated.

He'd come up with photographic evidence that proved the connection between Doucette and the Colombians, as well as some new players in the game. The first thing Sloan did was to get a set of the photographs off to Washington for identification.

Shortly thereafter, Rogers, following a lead of his own, trailed cartel members and witnessed them meeting with an American—whom he knew. It was during this phase of the operation that Rogers sensed he'd been spotted. Though he retreated, it was with a growing sense of unease. As insurance he left a message on the lady cop's answering machine, informing her of his findings

Rogers found he had a message from Sloan, left at the drop they used, asking him to meet with an American specialist who was being brought in covertly to become involved in the investigation. Rogers had no idea why the American was coming in and he didn't ask. It wasn't his business. He simply did as Sloan requested, contacting the American and fixing a meet.

Still aware of being watched, the Jamaican tried to slip away from his apartment, but Doucette's goons were still waiting and caught up with him before he'd gone a couple of blocks.

They bundled Rogers into the back of a panel truck. He was bound hand and foot, and a cloth hood was pulled over his head. The ride that followed was long and uncomfortable.

He would have admitted to being frightened to anyone who might have asked. His fear was more to do with the unknown than anything else. The darkness of the ride, coupled with his helplessness, conjured up jumbled, terrifying images in the man's mind.

Journey's end brought no relief. From the dark of the panel truck he was thrust into yet another place of shadows, this one dominated by a hulking giant with slanted eyes.

And then Rogers's agony began. He had never given thought to whether he would be able to face the prospect of torture. The possibility became reality when the silent giant began his dreadful work. Rogers rapidly descended into his own personal hell. The natural world faded into a dark and bloody void. Naked and helpless, he slid into the maw of shrieking hurt.

He resisted at first—and resisted well—but the full horror of what was being done to his body finally broke his spirit.

He begged for release; for an end to the pain.

He promised his captors anything if they would only stop. If only they would let his mutilated flesh alone and allow the pain to subside.

But his tormentor was a past master at the art of persuasion. He could calculate exactly how far he needed to go before his victim would offer every scrap of information floating around inside his skull. So the pain continued, the ravaged flesh yielding to the tools of the torturer, until Rogers began to talk willingly and without further prompting.

Only then did the shadowy figures begin to ask their questions. They extracted all the information they required with ease. He was eager to give them everything he knew. The words tumbled from his shredded lips in a torrent. His willingness to talk became an obsession.

When the torrent slowed and Rogers lapsed into agonized silence, his mind pushed him into the realms of self-doubt and guilt.

Awareness of what he had said came flooding back. In his desperation he had betrayed his partners, had revealed information they had gathered, told of meeting places.

Regret tinged with shame overwhelmed him. He raged within at his personal weakness, at his abandonment of his unsuspecting partners now at risk.

He thought about the American who had recently arrived on the island, a man he had arranged to meet and who would now walk straight into a trap.

And face sudden death.

The soft click of a gun being cocked brought a rush of tears to Rogers's eyes. The thought of his own death made him realize that others might soon follow.

He felt the cold touch of steel against his flesh, and said a silent prayer, asking for forgiveness.

There was no sound. Only a blinding, numbing force that filled his skull. He seemed to fall back into an expanding, silent, total blackness. It closed around him, shutting out everything.

1

The night was alive with hostile guns, and their target was Mack Bolan. Once again the Executioner found himself in the line of fire.

The meet with a local contact had turned sour. Bolan's instinct for survival had warned him of a double cross at the last moment. That, and his fast reflexes, had saved him from the hail of bullets.

Now he was running for his life in a strange city, on an island paradise that had about-faced and become hell on earth.

Bolan had been in Kingston, Jamaica, only a day and a half. During that time his presence seemed to have generated enough concern for someone to put out a contract on him.

The alley that had only moments ago provided a safe haven for his meeting echoed to the blast of autofire. Needle chips of brick peppered the warrior's cheek as bullets hammered the wall. He half turned, the Beretta 93-R in his fist.

The dark outlines of the pair of assassins were approaching him, closing the distance. The gunners had held their fire until they were sure of their target.

Bolan gripped the 93-R in both hands, tracking the guy in the lead, then triggering a 3-round burst that split his enemy's skull. The hardman twisted in response to the stunning impact of 9 mm parabellum rounds, then pitched facedown in the dirt of the alley. Out of time and out of life.

The surviving gunner jerked up the autoweapon he was carrying, panic dictating his reactions. His finger jerked on the trigger, sending a wild stream of slugs through the gloom. They failed to come even close to Bolan. He dropped to a crouch, steadying the Beretta before releasing a second trio of 9 mm rounds. This burst plowed into the gunner's chest, knocking him back against the alley wall. He dropped his gun, moaned in a loud, trembling voice, hands clutched to his bloody body. Before the guy slid to the ground, Bolan had drifted away from the alley, cutting along the rear of the buildings, then emerging on the crowded, noisy street to mingle with the rubberneckers who had been attracted by the gunfire.

The Executioner stayed with the jostling crowd, standing beside a middle-aged American couple who were obviously tourists. He waited until the wail of sirens signaled the arrival of the local police before easing away from the crowd and wandering back to where he had left his rental car.

Once behind the wheel he sat for a few moments, watching the activity around the alley through his rearview mirror, then started the engine and eased away from the curb.

He had something to do before he returned to his hotel—he had to pay a visit to his contact man.

Bolan had been given two names for his Jamaican mission. One was an undercover DEA agent, the man who had generated the information that had brought Stony Man into the picture. The Executioner had been given details about the guy, but had been told that the DEA man would contact him when he thought it necessary.

The second name had belonged to a local Jamaican who was working with the DEA agent. Where the American had to keep a low profile, the Jamaican was able to work on a freer basis. On arrival in Kingston, after settling in, Bolan had contacted the man and arranged for a meet.

Now the meet had turned bad. Bolan was on the defensive, needing to know what had gone wrong and why. He had to find out how far his cover had been blown and who was out to terminate him.

The contact's name was Winston Rogers, a local who knew Kingston well. Bolan hoped he knew it well enough to be able to finger the people intent on ending the Executioner's career.

The warrior drove through town, heading for the man's home, which lay in the northern section of Kingston, on the fringes of a slum area. There was a lot of new construction taking place in the neighborhood, and eventually Rogers's street would be razed to the ground. That was in the future. Until then the district would continue to house those not able to pay the high prices for fashionable homes. It was rife with crime and poverty, and designated a no-go area for tourists. Bolan was no tourist, nor was he feeling in a holiday mood. Anyone who crossed his path was liable to feel the Executioner's anger.

Bolan drove by construction sites, silent now, the partially constructed buildings illuminated by security lights. As he rolled deeper into the area, he was able to see the grimmer reality of Jamaica's city slums. This was far away from the sun, sand and gaiety of the Jamaican vacation front. Here was a country struggling to maintain its economy in the face of rising unemployment and still having to depend to a large extent on its tourist industry. The situation was ripe for exploitation. The poor, with little hope on the horizon, were easy prey for the criminal fraternity. It was a picture Bolan had seen many times, in many parts of the world: the weak and helpless falling under the shadow of organized crime.

The warrior halted the car on a street that had seen better days, feeling the tires crush the trash that lined the gutter. Sitting behind the wheel, he studied his surroundings. Several dilapidated buildings in various stages of decay were boarded up, awaiting the bulldozers that would knock them down. Many, though, were still occupied. Lights shone behind grimy windows. Music blared from a number of the buildings, each wave of sound competing with the others. The music was all similar. Mostly reggae and performed by local groups.

Bolan stepped out of the car, locking the driver's door. He was conscious of being watched from the shadows, and was well aware that his presence in the neighborhood wouldn't be welcome. The fact did nothing to deter him. He had something to do that wouldn't wait. He moved along the sidewalk, heading for the gaudily lighted front of a pool hall. Rogers lived upstairs.

As he reached the entrance, Bolan heard footsteps close behind. He turned slowly and found himself confronted by three Jamaicans dressed in odd combinations of casual clothing. They regarded him with open hostility.

Bolan's silence threw them. They had been expecting a challenge. His refusal pushed the onus their way.

After a few seconds the obvious leader of the trio leaned forward and jabbed a long finger at Bolan.

"You ain't welcome here, Yank. Why don't you get your white ass back where it belong?"

The first point of interest as far as Bolan was concerned was that he had been called "Yank." He hadn't spoken, so his identity had to have been known to the Jamaicans. Someone had to have been expecting him to pay a call on Rogers, which indicated that his escape from the assassination attempt had reached the attention of those responsible for setting it up. Hence this welcoming committee.

"You deaf?" the Jamaican demanded. He was starting to show a nervous side to his character. "Maybe you better come along with us. We got people like to talk with you." When Bolan still didn't speak, the Jamaican gestured sharply to his companions.

The one on his left reached into a back pocket and produced a switchblade. He touched the button, and the slim blade snapped into place.

The guy on the other side made a move toward his back pocket.

Bolan began to raise his hands, as if he were backing off. The gesture held the trio for a brief moment. Long enough for the Executioner to explode into action.

His right foot swept up, the toe of his shoe driving in between the legs of the man on the right. The kick was delivered with Bolan's full force. The Jamaican let out a high, wailing scream, then doubled over on the dirty sidewalk, clutching his injured body.

As the warrior recovered from the move, pivoting toward the guy with the knife, the Jamaican lunged at him, spitting obscenities. His maneuver was hurried, with little grace, and Bolan judged him to be nothing more than a street punk. The man was no knife fighter, but that didn't lessen the danger he presented. It was no time to worry about style, Bolan decided, dropping into a slight crouch, his arms extended. He watched his adversary's angry eyes, saw the tension mirrored there and spotted the glitter of agitation as the guy made his move. The switchblade caught distant lamplight along its edge as it cut through the air. Bolan saw it coming way off. He was ready in plenty of time, catching the wrist, twisting it and ducking in under the arm. With a smooth pull the warrior dragged the arm over his shoulder, levering down hard. The bone snapped with a soft sound, ripping a pained screech from the Jamaican's lips. He slid to his knees, sobbing unashamedly.

Reaching under his jacket, Bolan pulled the Beretta and jammed the muzzle against the glistening cheek of the trio's leader as the guy tried to run by him. He caught hold of the man's gaudy shirt and swept him around in a half circle, slamming the Jamaican against the front of the building. He stared at Bolan, his eyes wide with fear.

The warrior shoved the muzzle of the 93-R under the guy's chin.

"You were saying?" the Executioner asked.

"Nothin', man. We made a mistake."

"We're both agreed about that," Bolan said. "What I'd like to know is who got you to make yours?"

The man fell silent. He wasn't about to reveal his employer's identity.

"Let's go and have a talk with Winston Rogers," Bolan suggested. "Maybe he can answer my question."

"Winston ain't here, man. You're too late. He's gone. Tomorrow they goin' to find him floatin' in the ocean. What's left of him."

Anger boiled inside Bolan. Something in the Jamaican's tone revealed the truth in his words. Knowing that Rogers was the warrior's contact, the opposition had made certain he wouldn't be able to pass along any information. With Rogers dead, Bolan had been next. The trio of Jamaican toughs had been employed to take care of that. The people he was up against had something worth killing for, and the cost was rising by the minute.

Bolan stepped back from the Jamaican. Released from the Executioner's grip, the guy sagged against the wall. He seemed to have regained a little of his confidence as he glanced at his former quarry, smiling slightly.

"Like I said, Yank, it ain't too healthy for you in Kingston. This not your damn business. Go home before you die, too. Bein' nosy was Winston's problem. He been lucky for a long time. He get too clever for his own good and now he dead."

Bolan put away the Beretta. He wasn't going to get much cooperation from the Jamaican, and the open sidewalk wasn't the place to argue the matter. Maybe there was another way to draw the opposition's interest.

"Tell your boss, whoever he is, that I'm on his tail. And he'd better watch his back because I'm going to be there. Do it, then stay out of my way. Next time I see you, brother, I'll finish what I started here tonight."

Turning away, Bolan returned to his parked car. He climbed in, started the engine, made a U-turn and sped away, heading back to the center of Kingston and his hotel.

Moments later the warrior parked his car and made his way into the hotel. He picked up his key, took the elevator to his floor, then strolled to his room. Unlocking the door, he went in, closing it behind him.

As he was about to touch the light switch, something made him pause. He stared into the semidarkness of the room, feeling the hairs on the back of his neck prickle.

He wasn't alone.

Someone was in his room.

Bolan reached for the Beretta, fingers closing around the butt.

A light switch clicked and the bedside lamp burst into life, spreading its glow across the double bed.

It also illuminated the man sitting on the bed's edge, the automatic pistol in his right hand aimed at Bolan's chest.

"Leave the gun," the man ordered. "You won't be needing it this time. Come on over. We've got a lot to talk about, Mike Belasko."

2

"Ed Sloan," the man said by way of introduction, "DEA. I believe you were told about me."

Bolan moved into the room, still cautious. Sloan had addressed the Executioner by his cover name, but too much had happened in one night to make him accept anything at face value. He watched Sloan put away his weapon.

"I was told you're a hard guy to convince," the agent said. "All I can do is give you the name of the man in Washington who dealt with my boss."

Bolan waited.

"The guy I report to is Jack LeGault. He arranged for you to be involved via a top Fed named Hal Brognola."

The Executioner sat down, eyeing Sloan. Everything the man had said tallied, he fit the description Brognola had given him.

"Okay."

"You look like you've had a hard night," Sloan remarked.

Bolan nodded. In a few short sentences he gave the man a rundown on the night's events. Sloan listened in silence.

There was something in the agent's expression that prompted a question from the Executioner.

"How well did you know Rogers?"

"He put in some good time for me," Sloan replied. "Took a lot of risks getting information for my case. He was a nice guy. That's all I can say."

"I'm sorry it ended the way it did for him," Bolan said. "The hell of it is they might have given him a bad time getting information about our meet. Someone's playing for keeps."

"Can't say I'm surprised. This bunch has been getting pretty jumpy the past week or so. My guess is they've got something big set to go."

"Any idea what?" Bolan asked.

Sloan shook his head. "Nothing definite. All I'm certain of is it's got to do with more than just drugs. There are too many faces around town that don't normally fit in with the Colombians."

"How long have you been working this case?"

The DEA agent grinned. "Too damn long. Is it starting to show? There are times I forget who I really am. No kidding, Belasko, I can't wait to get back home."

Bolan knew what the man meant. He spent so much time walking the killing grounds himself it became too easy to lose track of his real identity. He existed in a permanent state of full alert, on the move, chasing around the world on mission after mission. In the Executioner's case, however, that condition was self-inflicted. He had dedicated himself to his eternal war so long ago it seemed unreal. How many miles had he moved forward since Pittsfield? There were times it totaled numbers too high to count. On other days when he looked around the ravaged world he didn't believe he'd taken a single step. But whatever the sum of his achievements, Bolan never once even considered stopping. He couldn't. Because if he did the battle was lost.

"You want to fill me in on what you've got?" the Executioner asked.

"Three months ago we picked up on a rumor about the Colombians moving into Jamaica. We followed up on it and confirmed Colombian movement in the area. That was where I came in. My speciality is deep cover. I came over here and started to gather info. We had a contact on the island with Winston Rogers, so I wasn't starting cold. But we had to move damn slow. I tagged a few familiar faces, then some new ones and was building my file. Then I started picking up on something odd. Passed it back to Washington and next thing I knew I was told you were coming in."

"What was the odd stuff you spotted?" Bolan asked for clarification.

"I pinpointed where the Colombians were based and got a sniff of how they were planning to get their drugs into the States. Both link up. It's all down to a company called Cross Brothers Inc., a big Jamaican company with all kinds of interests. They have a mining division that digs up bauxite and ships it to the U.S."

Bauxite was an ore that was plentiful on Jamaica, and was the source of much of the island's economy. The ore was a vital element in the manufacture of aluminum, and the bulk of the island's production was sent to America. Bauxite meant big business to Jamaica, and big business meant money flowing into the economy.

"I've got a hunch that the Colombians are tied in with somebody in the company. I'm pretty sure they're going to use the ore ships to smuggle the drugs through to the U.S. What I also hit on was the fact that the Colombians have some kind of HQ up in the Blue Mountains. They're based in a luxury house complete with its own grounds. The place is sewn up tight, but I did manage to sneak a look with high-powered binoculars. They've got armed guards, and even a helicopter pad. They've got a bunch of people up there who don't look like Colombians any more than you or I do."

"Meaning?"

Sloan shrugged. "Hard to explain, Belasko. These white guys are a hard-looking bunch. They're more than just heavies with guns. Nothing like the kind of muscle the Colombians usually hire to scare the hell out of people. I don't know what they're planning up there, but it's certain sure not a beach party."

The agent's explanation tied in with the intel Brognola had given Bolan during his short briefing. The big Fed had been explicit in his instructions to the Executioner. Bolan's mission was to infiltrate the Colombians' setup, find out what they were doing and put it out of action.

"With all respect to the DEA," Brognola had explained, "I think we need your specialist skills out there, Striker. We need to know about this other business. If the Colombians are trying for a Jamaican setup, we want it out of action. For good. You know how the President feels about the cartels. This has got to be done hard and fast.

"The Navy will get you ashore from a submarine. Your Belasko cover will be in place. Passport and all relevant papers and visas have been prepared. It has to be done this way in case the Colombians have any Jamaicans on their payroll. The less they know the better at this stage. If anything falls apart, the President is prepared to intervene."

"You got any hard information for me?" Bolan asked the DEA agent. "Locations? Pictures?"

Sloan nodded. He took a manila envelope from his jacket and passed it to Bolan.

"There's also the address of my place. If you need me, or just want a place to crash, you're welcome to use it."

Bolan nodded. "Thanks, Sloan."

"Hey, the name's Ed."

The warrior slipped the envelope into his pocket, then pushed to his feet. He was crossing the floor, extending his hand to the DEA man when the night exploded in his face.

There was a crash of breaking glass, and the curtains over the window billowed inward. Something thudded to the floor, a dark, spherical object.

Bolan's mind registered it instantly.

A grenade.

"Hit the floor!" he yelled at Sloan.

The Executioner dived for the far side of the bed, landing hard, rolling.

He heard the thump of Sloan's feet, realizing in that instant that the DEA man had rolled off the bed on the same side as the grenade.

"Ed..." he called.

His words were blown out of existence as the grenade detonated, filling the room with its sound and fury. The blast hammered at Bolan's senses. He felt the floor shudder, and it felt as if everything in the room were moving. Debris rained down on him, glass shattered, objects crashed against the walls, tumbled, hit the floor.

Bolan had the Beretta in his hand again as he stood up, peering through the haze of smoke that lay like a gauzy curtain across his vision. He looked at the window.

His mind clicked back into gear. A grenade meant someone around to throw it, and that person might look for bodies.

The warrior was right. As he focused on the window, he saw a hand reach through the gap in the curtains and thrust them aside. A dark face showed, followed by shoulders and an arm that held a large-caliber autopistol.

Bolan, on his knees, tracked the intruder. He triggered the sound-suppressed Beretta, drilling a trio of 9 mm parabellum slugs into the guy's chest. The rounds burned into flesh and shattered bone, the impact shoving the man back out the window to crash onto the metal fire escape.

There was an angry yell and the clatter of feet on the metal ladder. Bolan figured there were more hardmen on the way. It was time he moved on.

He cast a swift look in the direction of Ed Sloan's motionless body. There was no need for a closer look. The DEA agent had stepped directly into the grenade's blast. His body had been reduced to a pulpy, bloody wreck. His face was unrecognizable.

Bolan searched for his suitcase. It lay on the floor, torn to shreds, the contents ruined. Turning away, he opened the door and slipped out of the room. He could hear raised voices and the sounds of movement in adjoining rooms. In seconds the corridor was going to be full of curious rubberneckers. He needed to be gone before they showed up.

When he had checked in, the warrior had located the emergency exit at the end of the corridor. It lay two doors from his room. Without a moment's hesitation he ran for the door and hit the bar. The door swung open and Bolan stepped through. He raced down four flights of stairs, then eased open the fire door that allowed him access to the outside.

Moments later he was walking along the street, away from the hotel. Behind him he could hear the approach of police cars, their sirens blaring. Keeping his pace steady, Bolan cut across two more streets, then hailed a cab and directed the driver to take him to the address he had memorized from the envelope Ed Sloan had given him.

He hadn't anticipated taking up the DEA man's offer of a place to stay so soon. But at the moment he had nowhere else to go, and he needed some breathing room to figure out his next move.

3

The cab dropped Bolan at the end of the street where Sloan had lived. It was tree-lined and pleasant, the large houses relics of the island's colonial past. Too costly to maintain, they had been converted into apartments.

Bolan stood in the shadows of a tall tree, his eyes searching the apparently empty street. He took his time, thoroughly checking the area before he moved down the sidewalk. He reached the house without incident, walking quickly up the path and inside the front door. Sloan's apartment was on the second floor. Bolan had to force the door, which didn't prove too difficult. Once inside he snapped the security bolt into place.

The apartment consisted of a large living room, with a neat kitchen situated behind a breakfast bar. Directly across from the door were French windows that opened onto a balcony overlooking the street. There was a single bedroom off the main area, and next to that was a bathroom. Bolan was able to view the layout without switching on a light, as the apartment was partially lighted by the glare of the streetlights.

The Executioner drew the curtains across the French windows, making sure they were secure. Then he crossed to the breakfast bar and switched on the strip light fixed there, which provided enough light for him to locate a coffeemaker and coffee. While the brew percolated, the warrior sat at the breakfast bar and went through the information in the envelope Sloan had given him.

The intel consisted of a number of postcard-size monochrome photographs. On the rear of each photograph was a description of the images.

Bolan spread the pictures out before him, studying each carefully and committing faces and names to memory. Sloan had produced excellent shots. The faces in the photographs were sharp and clear.

As the DEA agent had explained, there were faces that didn't seem to fit. Bolan sorted out the nationalities himself. The local Jamaicans were easy to identify, as were the Colombians.

The interesting images belonged to half a dozen Caucasians. They could have been Americans, European or British. One of them figured in three of the photographs, a tall, leanly muscular man with a cold expression in his eyes. Bolan assessed him as someone high up within the group. He had, even in a still photograph, a commanding image. He looked hard, ruthless even. The warrior's keen scrutiny took note that whenever the cold-eyed man appeared, there was always another man with him. He was in the background, unobtrusive yet making his presence felt by those around him. This background figure was broad and bulky. He had an Oriental look to him, his black hair cut very short against his wide skull. Korean, Bolan judged, most likely a bodyguard, which added to his assumption that the cold-eyed man was some kind of leader.

Accepting that, the natural question was—leader of what?

Bolan went over the pictures again and again, searching for a clue to what the group was up to, why these people were on the island.

The Colombians often employed foreigners, and it was well documented that British ex-military men had been in the pay of the traffickers. The Britons had trained Colombian gunmen. Bolan had also heard of other mercenaries, U.S., French, Israeli, who had jumped on the lucrative cartel bandwagon. Maybe the Colombians had brought some of their mercs with them to Jamaica. There would be a need for the traffickers to have local enforcers on the streets, and Jamaicans, well trained, would blend in with the local scene easier than white hardmen.

He heard the percolator bubble, indicating that the coffee was ready. The Executioner left the photographs, poured himself a mug of coffee, then wandered around the apartment.

The muted sound of a car in the street attracted his attention. He eased a corner of the curtain aside and peered through the window. The car rolled by the house. It was a light-colored sedan of British manufacture. Bolan watched the vehicle cruise along the street, saw the taillights wink as it reached the corner, turn and vanish. A minute later the car turned back onto the street and moved in the direction of the apartment house.

The Executioner clicked to defensive mode. He crossed to the breakfast bar, collected the photographs and slid them into his jacket pocket. Then he killed the light, drew the Beretta and moved to the door. Opening it, Bolan glanced along the hallway. It was empty at the moment.

He went down the stairs two at a time, watching the corridor that led to the front entrance. He had no thoughts of using that way out. At the bottom of the stairs he cut along the hallway toward the rear of the building, counting on there being a back door. The far end of the hall took him to a laundry room, where a couple of washing machines stood against the wall. The door he located opened onto the apartment building's backyard.

In the distant past it had been someone's pride and joy. Now the area was untended and overgrown. Tall grass fought for space with weeds. The area was bounded on three sides by a high brick wall.

Bolan plunged through the grass, feeling burrs snatch at his clothing as he made for the far wall. He jammed the Beretta into its holster, leaving both hands free. As he neared the wall, he gathered himself, taking a muscle-powered leap for the top edge. His fingers caught, his weight dragging against his arms. As he hauled himself to the top of the wall, he made out a narrow lane running along the backs of adjoining properties. Without pause he rolled off the wall, landing lightly, then cut off along the lane.

The warrior heard shouts behind him. Glancing over his shoulder, he saw dark figures coming over the wall. They were on his trail.

Bolan drew the Beretta as he ran. His mind raced, seeking a solution to his predicament. He might outrun them, but would he be able to lose them? His main problem was that he didn't know the lay of the land. This was unknown territory for the Executioner. Circumstance had placed him here before he had been given the chance to do a proper recon. It left him with the problem of knowing which way to head, and ultimately could cost him his life.

The opposition was on home turf. Prior knowledge gave them the advantage, the chance to take paths that might get them ahead of Bolan.

There was a conspiracy taking place in Jamaica. Bolan had stirred up a hornet's nest by his intrusion, and because of that two men were already dead. In the Executioner's book that was two too many. Any sudden, violent death was unfortunate. It was doubly so when those who lost their lives were men working for the good of the majority. Men like Ed Sloan, who spent years living in the shadows, building fake identities so they could move among the predators and cancel out their evil schemes. Sloan had paid the ultimate price for his work. In his way, Winston Rogers had been akin to Sloan, living on the edge, sifting and passing along information. Always with the risk of being caught. And being caught meant paying the highest price.

The two dead men weighed heavily on Bolan's shoulders. He was strong enough to carry that burden. Aware that each man would have accepted what he was putting at risk didn't make it any easier. All the warrior could do was to ensure that Sloan and Rogers didn't die for nothing.

To do that he needed to stay alive himself.

The roar of a car engine reached his ears. The bouncing headlights of the vehicle appeared at the far end of the lane. The vehicle bumped and bounced over the rough ground, picking up speed as it swept in the Executioner's direction.

Bolan kept on running. He had no choice. His pursuers were still behind him, closing fast. He had been expecting them to open fire any second and assumed they were holding off now because of the car. If they missed Bolan, they might hit the vehicle.

The solution popped into his mind unbidden, and Bolan acted on it without further deliberation.

He dropped to one knee, his left hand flipping down the front handgrip situated under the Beretta's barrel. It enabled him to hold the weapon steady for a precise shot. Leveling the pistol, Bolan sighted in on the approaching car. He counted down the numbers as they fell away, knowing he only had seconds in which to act.

The Beretta chugged out its 3-round burst. The car's left headlight blew and went black. Switching his aim, Bolan took out the right light. The shattering glass left the driver without illumination. He jammed on his brakes, slowing the car almost to a halt as he tried to adjust his eyes to the sudden gloom.

Bolan sprang to his feet, sprinting hard for the car before it moved off again.

As he cut to the side of the vehicle, the passenger door swung open. The guy climbing out tried to bring his handgun into play as Bolan lunged by the car. The Executioner lifted his right foot and slammed it against the door, driving it into the gunner's body. The guy was hammered back against the doorframe, grunting in pain.

The Executioner caught hold of the guy's hair, snapping his head against the sharp edge along the top of the door, then thrust him aside. He sensed movement inside the car and twisted his body away from the open door as the driver leaned across the seat and triggered a shot at him. The bullet clipped the sleeve of the warrior's coat.

Two 3-round bursts from the Beretta burned into the driver's body, punching him lifeless against his own door.

Bolan ejected the near-exhausted clip, dropping it into his pocket and ramming home a fresh one.

Using the car door as a shield, he picked out his pursuers. He counted three of them.

An autoweapon opened up. The car shuddered as a hail of slugs pounded the bodywork. Window glass shattered, showering Bolan with glittering shards. Anticipating that the attackers would separate, he leaned out from behind the door and tracked in on the most visible. He fired off a 3-round burst, catching the guy high in the chest. The would-be killer crashed to the ground, his world abruptly awash with pain.

Bolan turned and crouch-walked to the rear of the vehicle moving around the trunk to the opposite side. He caught the second of the attackers coming along the side of the car. Bolan rose slightly, leveling the 93-R and triggering a burst that ended the guy's murderous plans in a blaze of agony.

The survivor opened up with his autoweapon, raking the car from hood to trunk. His action was prompted by a combination of anger and fear. It was a rash decision, allowing his emotions to control him in a combat situation. He paid the price the moment his weapon clicked empty. Throwing it aside, the gunner snatched his holstered autopistol from shoulder leather, gripping it two-handed as he stalked his elusive prey.

Bolan rose from his prone position on the ground, leaned across the riddled trunk and caught the guy dead to rights. There was no hesitation in the warrior's move. He locked on to his target and pulled the trigger, drilling a trio of 9 mm slugs into his adversary's chest. The guy fell back, his handgun spinning from nerveless fingers as he struck the dusty ground and kicked away his final seconds on earth.

The Executioner checked the area before he moved, wary of any backup guns waiting in the shadows. His instincts fueled his caution. Too many overconfident men had died simply because they had lowered their guard before checking the combat zone.

Even as he carried out his checks, Bolan knew he was on fairly safe ground. The force he'd been up against were killers, sure, but they were far from being seasoned in true combat. These were street soldiers, nothing more, like the ones in the alley and outside Winston Rogers's place. They most likely belonged to the same organization that had carried out the attack on his hotel room. Dangerous people, yes, but not trained and disciplined any further than their business required. Even so, Bolan took his time, assuring himself he was in the clear before he made a body count, checking for any ID. He found nothing except the normal contents of pockets. There was nothing to give him any indication who his attackers had been, or who they worked for.

The only certain fact was the one that told him *someone* wanted him dead.

Keeping to the deeper shadows along the base of the wall that ran the length of the lane, Bolan left the kill zone. He could hear background noise as people in the neighboring houses reacted to the gunfire. Lights began to show in windows, doors opened. It wouldn't be long before the area was swarming with curious onlookers, and eventually the police. The Executioner wanted to be far away before that happened.

He reached the end of the lane. The road stretching away in both directions was poorly lighted, and deserted. Bolan turned left, heading away from the residential area. First chance he got he'd flag a taxi and find someplace to stay. He needed breathing space, somewhere that would allow him to formulate his next move.

He had been walking for a few minutes when he became aware of being followed. Without breaking stride he took a covert glance over his shoulder. A car was behind him, driving without lights, and keeping pace with him.

Easing the Beretta from shoulder leather, Bolan flicked the selector to single-shot. He held the autopistol against his thigh as he continued walking, searching for a convenient breakaway spot.

The car's engine revved suddenly, tires squealing briefly as the vehicle accelerated.

Bolan tensed, starting to turn, the Beretta coming on line as he anticipated hostile moves from the vehicle's occupants.

Instead the car bore down on him, swerving at the last moment. The British-made Vauxhall Cavalier rolled alongside Bolan, and the passenger door swung open.

"Get in, Mr. Belasko, because I don't want to stay around here any longer than necessary. You've upset enough people already, and I have no intention of becoming embroiled in one of your shoot-outs.''

The speaker's tone implied a no-nonsense attitude, coupled with fierce determination. The accent was local and also female.

4

The woman behind the wheel was Jamaican and young, somewhere in her late twenties, Bolan judged. She was also beautiful, and totally capable of handling the car at high speed, which she demonstrated as she powered the vehicle along the dark road.

"I'm Lisa Raymond, Mr. Belasko," she said by way of introduction. "Detective Sergeant, Kingston Constabulary. I've been working undercover alongside Ed Sloan for the past couple of months."

"Then I guess you know what's been happening tonight," Bolan stated.

Raymond nodded. Her expression hardened. "I was waiting outside the hotel when the grenade exploded. By the time I got inside it was all over. I recognized Ed by the clothes he was wearing. As soon as I realized you weren't there, I left and drove out to Ed's place."

"What made you do that?" Bolan asked.

The woman smiled at his suspicious question. "Ed told me he was going to pass some information to you to bring you up-to-date on the investigation. He also said he would give you his address so you'd have a safehouse to go to in case of trouble."

"Trouble's been the byword since I set foot on this island. Either the opposition is better informed than I figured, or Sloan's security was slack."

Raymond's reaction was instant and dramatic. She jammed her foot on the brake and brought the car to a controlled, speedy stop. The woman's face was taut with anger as she turned to face Bolan.

"Ed Sloan was too good to allow slack security, Mr. Belasko. As far as I'm concerned, he did it by the book, and he did it bloody well. Whatever went wrong can't be laid at Ed's door. Because if it was his fault, then he's paid a pretty high price for it, hasn't he?"

Her outburst was genuine, her feelings for Sloan strong. Mack Bolan felt he was a good judge of character, and he was convinced that Lisa Raymond's defense of Ed Sloan was from a close association with the DEA agent. Bolan had needed to probe the lady cop in order to sound out her feelings. Brognola had insisted the Executioner be put into Jamaica covertly, so as not to alert any possible insiders who might tip off the Colombians. Raymond was a local, a police officer, and she had been close to Sloan. If he had harbored any suspicions about her, Bolan felt that they would have been unfounded. He was taking her on trust, knowingly accepting that by doing so he placed his life in her hands.

"Okay," he said gently. "I needed to know. For both our sakes."

Raymond relaxed, slumping back in her seat. She stared at her slim brown hands gripping the steering wheel. After a few moments she cleared her throat and turned to glance at Bolan.

"I guess I should apologize, too," she said. "I'm angry because Ed died and I couldn't do anything to help him, and I'm taking it out on you. I shouldn't be doing that because we're on the same side. It looks like you have every reason to be angry, what with everything against you since you got here. But you see Ed was the closest I've ever had to a real partner. I'm feeling really lousy."

"Hey, you have a right to," Bolan told her. "The time to worry is when you don't hurt after you lose someone close."

Raymond started the car and eased away from the soft shoulder. She drove steadily, under control again, but remained quiet. Bolan sensed her mood and gave the lady some space until *she* was ready to speak.

"I think we both suspected trouble was in the offing," the woman finally said. "There was tension in the air. You could feel it. Does that sound silly?"

The warrior shook his head. "Comes with the job. After a while your instincts tell you things are changing. That's the time when you watch your back."

"Obviously we didn't watch close enough. What set it off, Mr. Belasko?"

"The name's Mike. As to what set the ball rolling, I don't know. I'm inclined to go for Rogers. I was supposed to meet with him tonight. Instead I found a couple of hired guns waiting for me. There were others at his place. One of the things I learned was that Winston Rogers is dead.''

The expression that crossed Raymond's face made Bolan realize the news of Rogers's death had been a shock.

"How did it happen?" she asked, her voice soft and shaky.

"From what I picked up I'd say he was grabbed by the opposition and they got the information they wanted." Bolan hesitated, not wanting to inflict any more hurt.

"Do you think they hurt him to get it?" she asked, her voice hard-edged now.

Bolan nodded.

"Damn!"

"You knew Rogers?"

"Yes. I brought him into the team. He'd done work for the police department before. He was a good man. He knew his business."

Raymond glanced across at Bolan, studying him carefully for a moment.

"I have a feeling you hit those hired guns pretty hard."

"They left me no choice," he told her. "After that the whole deal fell apart. Somebody has a taste for blood, and I don't think they're satisfied yet."

"If that was an attempt at scaring me, it worked. But being scared doesn't change my mind. I'm still assigned to this case and I intend sticking with it. I couldn't quit now even if I wanted to."

"I had a feeling you'd say that. Look, I need your help. Sloan's info on this group was sketchy. I'm inclined to agree with his view that they're something special, but what?"

"We hadn't figured that out," the cop replied. "We know the Colombians have been showing interest in the Caribbean as another way into the U.S. Sort of a back-door operation. There's a lot of movement between here and the mainland. Business and tourist. All of it good for the traffickers."

"Like the bauxite ships?"

Raymond nodded. "We don't have any hard evidence yet. Our original intel came from Winston. But that was as far as it went, and there hasn't been time to follow up on it."

"I'll make that time," Bolan said. "I need a jumping-off point."

"You mean you'll go in yourself?"

"It's why I'm here."

"Aren't you worried about the risk?"

"I'll handle it."

"When will you do it?"

"When the time's right," Bolan told her.

"What can I do?" Raymond asked.

"More checking on the company Sloan mentioned. Anything and everything. If Sloan was right, there has to be a connection between the Colombians and someone in the company. That's what we need."

"All right. Anything else?"

"Something you might not want to think about," Bolan said. "There's the possibility of a leak within your department, somebody on the inside who might be able to feed information to the opposition."

"Ed's presence on the island was kept pretty quiet. The whole operation was deliberately low-key. We had very little contact with the department."

"Sloan's being here had to have been sanctioned by someone," Bolan said.

"It was," Raymond agreed. "But I can't believe the people involved would leak anything. What could they gain?"

As soon as she had uttered the words, Raymond checked herself, glancing sideways at Bolan.

"That was pretty naive of me," she admitted. "You don't have to be a street cop to be bought. Corruption reaches every level."

"Just remember that when you start checking around," Bolan told her. "People who let themselves be bought can get nasty if they find they've been exposed."

"I'm pretty good at watching my back. Since I made sergeant four years ago, I've worked vice. The drug squad. All the dirty operations in the book. I know the game and the rules."

"So did Ed Sloan," Bolan said quietly, just as a timely reminder to the lady that they were all mortal.

And expendable.

"Is there anything you need?" Raymond asked.

Bolan nodded. "I left my rental car outside the hotel. I've special equipment in the trunk."

"Give me the keys and I'll pick it up for you."

The Executioner handed her the keys and described the vehicle.

"I'm going to drop you off somewhere you'll be safe until I bring your gear. I can guarantee this place. It's my own safehouse. No one knows about it. I didn't even mention it to Ed."

"Where is this place?"

"A couple of miles outside Port Maria, on the A3. It's a small bungalow overlooking the sea. Off the road and out of sight. You can't see the lane leading to it unless you know it's there."

Bolan settled back in his seat, allowing himself to relax. It had been a long, hectic night. He needed a little time to reassess the mission and to recharge his batteries.

Whichever way he looked at it, Jamaica was heating up, and it had nothing to do with the climate.

While Bolan rested, Raymond drove steadily, guiding the car along the dark road. The journey took just over two hours, and the Executioner was roused from his catnap by the car slowing and rolling along a bumpy track. He glanced through the windshield and saw the gleam of the calm sea beyond close-growing trees and bushes. Raymond guided the car to the end of the narrow lane, bringing it to a stop outside a low wooden bungalow. She switched off the engine.

Bolan climbed out, stretching gratefully. He could smell the tang of the sea in the cool air. A faint breeze drifted in from the wide bay below the cliff on which the house stood.

"What do you think?" his companion asked. Standing beside the car, she was tall and slim.

"Nice hideaway," he commented as he followed her to the house.

She smiled. "It's why I bought it. I can come here when I'm off duty and just forget everything."

Raymond unlocked the door and they went inside. She pulled up a wide blind, exposing a window that overlooked the bay. Moonlight pushed away some of the shadows in the room. Moving to a small table, she struck a match and lighted a brass oil lamp. As she lowered the glass, the living room was filled with soft light.

"Make yourself comfortable."

She vanished into the small kitchen, and Bolan heard the faucet turn on.

He settled himself in a comfortable armchair, his mind alive with thoughts. As much as he wanted to, he was unable to rid himself of the image of Ed Sloan, dead and mutilated in the hotel room, and the knowledge that Winston Rogers was also dead. Someone, somewhere on the island, had to be held accountable for the two deaths. They would pay, sooner or later. Bolan would see to that.

"You like your coffee hot and black?" Raymond asked.

Bolan looked up to see her standing over him, holding out a mug of steaming liquid. He took it. The coffee was rich and strong.

"That's good," he said.

"I'll get back to Kingston, pick up your gear from your car and bring it back here." She glanced at her watch. "I should be back by dawn. You can use the bedroom to get some sleep."

She took another swallow of her own drink, then turned to go.

"Will do," Bolan said. "And you be careful."

She turned back to flash him a wide smile. "I always am."

5

Brett Hornaday's anger was showing by the time he replaced the telephone receiver. It was noticeable in the way he sat silently staring across the room. Immobile. The only sign of movement visible was a tight flexing of his jaw muscle.

Behind Hornaday's chair stood the monolithic figure of Shen, his Korean bodyguard. The powerful, muscular figure shadowed Hornaday wherever the man went, always within arm's length and ready to protect his employer at a moment's notice. Shen, who rarely spoke, was skilled in tae kwon do and tang soo do, which was a Korean variant on Shotokan karate. Shen had proved his worth a number of times. His size and bulk often fooled opponents into thinking the Korean would be slow to react. Nothing could have been further from the truth. In action he was a terrifying figure, and his ability to maim and inflict injury was unpleasant to observe. Those who had been present during his torture of the Jamaican, Winston Rogers, were liable to remember the incident for a long time.

Simon Spendloe, slumped in a comfortable lounger, nursing a tall, iced glass of fresh orange juice, recognized the signs. He had been associated with the ex-CIA agent for longer than he cared to remember, so he was able to spot the storm brewing. From past experience he knew it was advisable to stay silent and let Hornaday work it out of his system.

Across the far side of the room Jason Cabot, tall, lean and red-haired, glanced up from his skin magazine. He had been listening to Hornaday's conversation. Now he was itching to get the lowdown.

"Sounds like somebody fucked up," he commented airily. "That right, Brett?"

Spendloe sank in his lounger, wishing he was somewhere else. He watched Hornaday through half-closed eyes. "Great move, Cabot," he mouthed at the Briton.

Fortunately Hornaday didn't react. The expected outburst failed to materialize. Watching him, Spendloe saw that the man was leaning back in his swivel chair, staring at the silent telephone.

After some time Hornaday spoke. His tone was controlled, his words carefully chosen.

"It seems we do have a problem," he announced in his precise way. "A situation has arisen that needs handling quickly."

"It got to do with that snoop from the mainland Rogers shot his mouth off about?" Spendloe asked.

Hornaday nodded. "Santos chose to let the locals handle it. He figured it best if we stayed out of the frame. I felt he was wrong at the time. And the way the hometown boys have fucked up I was right to complain.''

"They didn't get the guy?" Cabot asked.

"No. But *he* took out the hit team. Both of them iced. Then he turned up at Rogers's place later and danced all over three more of Royal's soldiers.''

"Who is this bastard?"

"All we have is a name. Mike Belasko. Royal's idiots hit his hotel room in a later attempt. They tried to frag the guy, but all they did was blow away Sloan, the DEA agent.''

"At least he's out of our hair then," Spendloe said.

"Maybe. But our mystery man got away after putting a slug in another of Royal's goons.''

"And?" Spendloe prompted, certain that the story wasn't over.

"Royal's team tried to take this guy out when he turned up at Sloan's apartment. Instead Belasko took out the whole damn crew, then vanished.''

"This guy is good," Spendloe said. "You have to give him that. He's handled everything Royal has thrown at him and come out on top.''

"He's got my respect," Hornaday replied. "Our contact in the police department got a look at the empty shell cases from the bullets used to take out Royal's two shooters in town. They matched the cases from the guy shot at the hotel. They all came from the same gun. They're 9 mm subsonic slugs. Now there aren't too many of those around. I'll take odds that the same slugs will be found in the last bunch of Royal's boys who got totaled tonight.''

"So we got a guy running around town with blood in his eye," Spendloe said.

Hornaday replied with a grunt.

"How close is this guy to us?"

"Royal's guess is that he's working on the drug business. Our end of the deal is supposed to be off limits."

"What if it isn't?" Cabot queried. "Maybe we got blown. For all we know that DEA agent might have got a lead on us and passed it to this jerk."

Hornaday smiled mirthlessly.

"If you're right, you can say so long to your bonus. I haven't forgotten what that dumb shit Rogers spilled about Sloan having a bunch of photographs he'd taken. If it's true and they get in the wrong hands, we could be on the Most Wanted list."

"We going to handle this Lone Ranger ourselves?" Spendloe asked.

"Damn right," Hornaday snapped. "I've had it with these local cowboys. I laid it out to Santos. He calls off Royal and his reggae crew and puts us in charge. At the end of the day it's our asses on the line. I'm not about to leave mine to be covered by these Jamaican hotshots if the DEA did get something on us."

"So how do we find this guy?" Cabot asked.

"We figure it out," Hornaday said. "It's what we're being paid for. I have a feeling sooner or later this guy is going to find us. He's no beginner. Remember that.

Don't treat him like some hophead. This guy knows his business."

Cabot tossed aside his magazine. "Yeah, well, he isn't the only one, you know."

Spendloe leaned forward. "Hey, didn't Sloan have a local helper other than Rogers? Some female cop running errands for him?"

"Right." Hornaday reached for the telephone again and quickly dialed a number. "Time for that fat toad Lawrence to earn his money. He should know what his own cops are doing. If he can pinpoint her location maybe we can get a lead on this maverick."

Cabot's interest was growing with each passing moment. He was almost drooling at the thought of action.

"Give me his ass, Hornaday," he begged. "Let me show these local clowns how to do it right."

Hornaday held up a hand for silence as his police contact came on the other end of the line. With little preamble he told the contact exactly what he wanted and instructed the man to get back to him the moment he had any news. Cutting the connection, Hornaday replaced the phone.

"You want this guy, Cabot? You got him. Find him and take him out. I just want the guy dead. Neat and tidy."

Cabot smiled in anticipation.

"It's done," he said. "The bastard is already on his way to the morgue."

Spendloe watched the Briton leave the room. He couldn't help smiling. The cocky ex-SAS man was good at his job, but he was cursed with a loose mouth and vanity that quickly became a drag. Cabot, who had worked with Hornaday and Spendloe for more than three years, regularly allowed his overconfidence to take control when he should have been holding back. If it hadn't been for his excellence with weapons and close-combat fighting, Hornaday might have dumped him. But he allowed for the man's character flaws because of his skills.

"Nice to have such a modest guy around the place," Spendloe remarked.

"One day he'll meet someone who isn't going to be impressed by all his crap."

Brett Hornaday had a feeling that Cabot might well come up against such a man very shortly. The Briton was sure he was going to handle the guy he was after with ease. Hornaday had other thoughts. The new player in the game had already shown that he was above the norm. The way he had handled each situation he came upon spoke of a true professional. Perhaps even more. Hornaday hadn't seen the guy but he knew him. The man was a soldier in the true sense of the word. Someone to be reckoned with. He was going to present the cartel with a hard fight, and Cabot would be the first of Hornaday's group to face up to him.

Leaning back in his seat, Hornaday reviewed the overall situation. He had a number of priorities. One of which was Rio Santos, the Colombian in charge of the Jamaican operation. Hornaday didn't like Santos. The guy was a pain. It was only because he was the favored nephew of one of the cartel's top honchos that he'd been given the Caribbean deal. Santos lacked experience in the field, and that could be fatal in the drug business. It took a leader with a sharp brain and sharper eyes to stay ahead of the game. As far as Hornaday was concerned, Santos wouldn't make it. Which was a shame. Because the Jamaican operation could be made workable, given the correct handling. There was a lot of mileage to be had out of this area. Santos, with his expensive tastes in clothes and cars, flashy women and loose spending, appeared to be somewhat of a liability. He was too far removed from reality. In the case of the drug business, reality meant hard business and a ruthless streak that was razor-sharp. Santos didn't have that.

Which was where Hornaday came in. He had built himself a solid, dependable reputation over the years. His work as a mercenary, which had taken him around the world, was well-known within his circle of acquaintances. Hornaday was a man who got the job done, with a minimum of fuss and who never broadcast his intentions or crowed about his success. When he had been approached by the cartel in Medallín, its offer had interested him immediately. The bosses wanted him to set up training programs for their enforcers, to establish bases deep in Colombia where the traffickers' troops could be taught the skills of both jungle and urban warfare. Hornaday's CIA background had left him with working knowledge of many security agencies, which he was able to pass on to his trainees. He also had invaluable contacts, giving him access to dealers in weapons and equipment of all kinds. Within six months of accepting the cartel's offer, Hornaday was running the whole show.

His insight into the workings of the DEA made it relatively easy for his people to keep one step ahead of the agency. It was made easier due to the fact that the DEA, though supposedly allowed a free hand in the drug wars, was still shackled by legal restraints. There was little its personnel could do on a practical basis without all the legal technicalities first being covered. Which meant wasted time and eventually lost cases. It was frustrating for the hardworking DEA agents, many of whom spent long months gathering evidence, only to have it thrown out because of some minor legality.

There were the other setbacks, too. Even if the DEA did get a judgment in its favor, oftentimes it proved difficult to lay hands on a trafficker who fled the U.S. and returned home to Colombia. Even so, the DEA was a constant irritation to the cartels. Every so often the agency got lucky and tagged a dealer, or made a big narcotics bust. Although the net result was small, the cartel didn't like it. And recently there had been some covert action against the cartels, hitting home in Colombia itself as well as in Miami. The overall operation had bitten deep, costing the cartels a lot of money and had damaged their reputation for being able to look after themselves.

One of Hornaday's tasks in the Jamaican operation was the establishment of his team as a hit squad. It would be their job to take out anyone causing problems for the cartel. His people would travel to mainland U.S.A. if required. As the Americans had decided to take the war to Colombia, Hornaday would return the compliment by striking at the heart of the U.S. administration.

The operation was only just getting off the ground. Hornaday had been assigned his first hit. Before he allowed himself to concentrate on that, he wanted to clear the decks by getting rid of the mystery man who was running around the island taking out Royal Doucette's men. Hornaday had too much riding on the Caribbean venture to let something like this put a black mark on his record.

6

Bolan woke suddenly. Alert in seconds, he reached for the loaded, cocked Beretta on the bedside table.

He sat up, glancing at his watch. It was almost 8:00 a.m. Morning sunlight forced its way through the closed slats of the blind over the bedroom window. Swinging his legs over the edge of the bed, he bent and slipped on his shoes. Even as he performed this mundane task his mind was searching for the elusive thing that had awakened him. He couldn't put his finger on it, but he felt certain his instinctive sense of danger had alerted him.

The Executioner crossed the bedroom, pausing at the door to listen. The house exuded silence. Maybe he was imagining things. He passed the bathroom, backtracked and stepped inside. Tucking the 93-R in the holster of the shoulder rig he was still wearing, Bolan bent over the washbasin and ran cold water on his hands, quickly sluicing his unshaved face. He dried himself with a towel and ran his fingers through his black hair as he moved on to the kitchen. He located a kettle and filled it, placing it on the small gas stove.

He found a match and lighted the ring under the kettle.

The warrior moved around the house restlessly. He felt a nervous energy building up inside him. He checked his watch.

Where was Lisa? Was she on her way back or had she been spotted and stopped? Even killed? Questions darted around the Executioner's skull, questions with no answers.

He made coffee when the kettle boiled. He drank two large cups of the hot, black liquid and was reaching to pour a third when the sound of an approaching car reached his ears. The sound was familiar.

Lisa's car.

Bolan slipped into his leather jacket and stepped outside as Lisa Raymond's car rolled to a halt. He watched her climb out, pulling his zippered carryall along with her. She smiled tiredly at him as she handed the bag to him.

"There's some fresh coffee inside," he said.

Her smile widened as she moved to join him.

"You sleep okay?" she asked.

Bolan nodded. His eyes were reaching beyond her, scanning the landscape, searching the sky. He felt certain they weren't alone. He reached out to take her arm and lead her inside.

"Ask me if I had a busy night," she said. Then not waiting, she continued. "Yes, I did. And I have some information you are going to be interested in. There was a message on my answering machine when I checked my Kingston apartment. From Winston. He must have called just before he was snatched. I could hear it in his voice. He was agitated, not himself. But he gave me a name. The guy working for Cross Brothers who's thrown in with the Colombians. Remember the name—Robert Johnson. Hey! Are you listening? I spent all—''

The sound of churning rotor blades reached Bolan's keen ears seconds before the dark shape of a helicopter swept into view above the waving treetops. The hovering craft held its position for long seconds then dipped suddenly, coming at them.

''Find cover,'' Bolan yelled above the racket.

Raymond stared at him, her eyes wide with surprise.

''Mike, I'm sorry, I didn't know they'd followed me.''

''Forget it and move!''

The chatter of a light machine gun was added to the roar of the chopper's engine. The ground erupted, whipped to dust as slugs chewed across the earth. Raymond's car rocked as slugs punched through the bodywork. Glass shattered, tires burst. The bullets changed course, tracking Bolan and the woman as they broke away from the house and made for the thick shrubbery on the far side of the building. The helicopter dropped lower, angling across the ground, the machine gun still hammering out its death load.

Bolan felt slugs gouging the ground close to his feet. He kept running, knowing that cover would be his only salvation.

He was aware of Lisa Raymond close at his side, her long legs driving her forward. She had drawn her handgun in readiness for any confrontation. The action proved to be worthless.

They were yards from the mass of greenery when the Jamaican woman gave a startled cry and threw her arms skyward. Her momentum kept her moving forward, despite the fact that she had caught a burst of machine-gun fire in her upper back.

Bolan made a grab for her with his free hand, gripping a handful of her clothing. He hauled her upright, guiding her toward the shrubbery where they both crashed through the tangled greenery and sprawled facedown on the ground. The gunfire continued as the chopper howled over their heads, out beyond the headland and over the bay. It began a tight turn, intending to come back for a second strafing run.

The warrior turned to his companion, rolling her over on her back. Her clothing was soaked with blood. More streaked her face and throat. She stared at Bolan, her expression full of regret.

"Mike, I didn't know they were on to me. If I had, I would have taken them miles away from here."

"It doesn't matter, Lisa. Just take it easy."

"Cut it out, Mike, I'm dying and we both know it. Just get yourself away from here fast."

"I can't just leave you."

"Oh, yes, you can." The woman suddenly gripped his hand. "Remember the name. Robert Johnson."

The chopper returned with a deep roar, darkening the sky above Bolan's head. The machine gun opened up, the gunner raking the shrubbery in a methodical pattern. It was only a matter of time before the line of slugs reached Bolan and Raymond.

"Can you stand up?" Bolan asked.

"No chance, Mike. Please, just go. Both of us dead isn't going to help matters. Just promise me you'll deal with these bastards. Get them off my island."

Her speech was starting to slur, words tumbling over one another. She was slipping into a coma, life ebbing away with the loss of her blood. Bolan stared at her, knowing full well there wasn't a thing he could do for her. He was helpless, angry, bitter at the waste of her young life.

From the far side of the bungalow he heard the roar of a car's engine—backup for the chopper. Bolan unzipped the carryall and withdrew the 9 mm Uzi machine pistol. He cocked the weapon, rezipped the bag and slung it over one shoulder.

He turned as he caught the approach of running feet, heard the rustle of foliage as the newcomers reached the shrubbery. He could hear their shouted orders as they parted company, digging into the greenery.

Bolan half rose, seeking his opponents, and found himself facing a startled Jamaican. The guy carried a

Heckler & Koch MP-5. The moment he spotted Bolan the gunner started to swing his weapon into play.

The Executioner's Uzi crackled sharply, firing a burst of 9 mm slugs that destroyed the Jamaican's features and dumped him ungracefully on the ground.

Another subgun opened up from Bolan's right. Bullets whipped through the shrubbery, shredding leaves and branches viciously. The warrior dropped to the ground, crawling away from his previous position. He watched the waving greenery as his opponent pushed his way through. The guy was ignoring all the rules of close combat, but Bolan wasn't about to put him right. When it came down to the killing game, survival was the thing. If the other guy made a mistake, that was his problem.

The man stepped into view, almost on top of Raymond. He dropped the muzzle of his Heckler & Koch and for no definable reason put a burst into her as she lay helpless before him.

Bolan saw red at the injustice of the man's act. He lunged forward, his Uzi arcing around to settle on the killer. A triburst drilled into the hardman's chest and throat. Screaming and spraying blood from his lacerated throat, the guy stumbled back. A second volley ripped his heart to shreds.

The chopper exploded into Bolan's life again, having completed its rapid turn. Once again the machine gunner began to hose the area below him. The heavy fire he laid down drove the Executioner deeper into cover. He concealed himself then lay still. He wasn't

about to commit the mistake of disturbing the greenery and providing the chopper's gunner with a clear
target area.

The gunfire stopped after a few long seconds, the
dark shape of the helicopter hovering above Bolan.
The aircraft swayed from side to side. Luckily for the
Executioner the rotorwash disturbed the foliage, con-
cealing any movement he might have made himself.
Even so it was a heart-stopping moment until the pilot decided he was wasting time and swept away for
another run.

The moment he was beyond the machine gun's arc
Bolan lifted the Uzi and raked the underside of the
chopper with a burst of 9 mm slugs. They ripped into
and through the thin aluminum fuselage, causing the
pilot to pile on the power and veer away.

Bolan crouched, watching and waiting. His keen
eyes searched the tangled greenery.

A shadow fell across his path. Bolan spun. He
caught a glimpse of a grinning white face, topped with
red hair.

"Bloody got you, chum," the man yelled. His accent was British and his manner overconfident.

The gleaming barrel of an automatic pistol swung
at Bolan's skull. He ducked, turning his body, and
caught the blow across his upper arm. It ripped a grunt
of pain from his lips, but failed to put him out of action. Bolan angled the Uzi and pumped a short burst
into his enemy's chest. The guy slumped to his knees,

falling forward, his deadweight pushing the Executioner backward.

The helicopter returned at that moment, the machine gunner loosing a short burst as it swept by. A stream of bullets chopped at the earth, reaching out for Bolan. They rose and caught the redhead, stitching a bloody track across his back. The impact shoved the guy hard against the warrior, but also protected him from the scything bullets.

Bolan thrust a foot behind him, hoping to regain his balance. It met empty air. As the dead man's limp form pushed him back another step, Bolan recalled the fact that Lisa Raymond's bungalow stood on the rim of the cliff overlooking the bay. His flash of insight was short-lived, cut off as he lost contact with solid ground and fell into space.

Bolan threw out a free hand, grasping at the clumped grass growing at the edge of the cliff. The tough roots held for a second, then tore free. A shower of dirt and stones cascaded down the uneven slope of the cliff, following the warrior as he crashed and bounced down in a dizzying spiral. The Uzi spilled from his hand and the carryall took on a life of its own. Clutching, grabbing, clawing, Bolan tried desperately to halt his dizzying descent. His own momentum and body weight worked against him. His breath was slammed from his lungs, as he slithered over eroded rocks. For a sickening moment he hung in midair, then dropped to hit the slope farther down.

The back of his head rapped against a slab of hard rock, and the bright Jamaican morning turned gray, then black. With the darkness came silence. Deep and complete.

7

The first sound Bolan heard was a distant pounding, a continuous noise that intruded over the duller ache of pain filling his skull. He moved slowly, aware of alternating cold and heat. Pushing his heavy eyelids open, he looked around, trying to make some sense from the fractured images wavering before him.

It took a little time for the warrior to realize he was lying facedown on a rocky ledge at the water's edge. The rise and fall of the Caribbean splashed over him every few seconds. He could taste the salt water on his lips.

Bolan sat up slowly. Caution dictated his actions. He wanted to be sure nothing was broken before he made a hasty move. He ached from head to foot. His descent down the steeply angled slope had left him with numerous cuts and scrapes. Apart from these he was in reasonably good shape. Once on his feet he turned to look back up the slope and realized he'd been lucky. This section of the cliff had been subjected to some kind of natural erosion. The subsequent fall of earth and rock had softened the face of the cliff, and had also softened Bolan's fall.

He searched the top of the cliff, suddenly remembering the less-than-friendly visitors. There was no movement up there. The sky was empty, as well. The roving helicopter seemed to have vanished, too.

Bolan reached for the holstered Beretta. To his relief the weapon still nestled in its holster. He took it out, feeling a little more secure. Stepping back from the water's edge, he cast around for his carryall and the Uzi he'd dropped. He was unable to find either. They could have gone into the water for all he knew. He spent a fruitless minute or two searching for them before deciding to cut his losses and move on.

He made his way along the rocky shore, eventually reaching a strip of white sand. From there he located a negotiable section of the cliff and began the long, slow climb to the headland.

Fifteen minutes later he was concealed in the shrubbery near the bungalow, checking the area. He neither saw nor heard anything. The house lay silent and deserted beneath the hot Jamaican sun. Lisa Raymond's car stood where she had left it, though the vehicle had been reduced to a bullet-punctured wreck by the helicopter's machine-gun fire.

Bolan moved in closer, taking his time, watching and listening. He reached the vehicle and crouched in its shadow. He peered in through the driver's window. There were no keys in the ignition, but if necessary he could hot-wire the vehicle.

Easing into the shrubbery, he checked the area where the firefight had taken place. Apart from broken shrubs and trampled grass, there was no physical evidence that anything had happened. No bodies remained. Even Lisa's had disappeared.

Bolan was about to return to the abandoned car when something caught his eye—a gleam of sunlight reflecting on glass hidden in the trees off the lane that led to the house. He studied the spot for a while, eventually making out the shape of a car parked out of sight. The moment he identified what was hidden there the Executioner retreated to cover.

The hit team—or part of it—was still around. The first question that popped into mind was why? If they had presumed him dead from the fall down the cliff, why were they still there? And where were they? Inside the house.

That had to be it.

They would be searching the place, anxious to find out whether Lisa Raymond had hidden any evidence of the investigation she and Ed Sloan had been working on. It seemed the most logical explanation to Bolan.

He eased his way closer to the house, ever watchful now in case there were any of them outside. He reached the end wall without encountering anyone. Pressed against the plank wall, the warrior listened intently and picked up the faint sounds of movement inside the building.

He moved around to the front. Pausing to put the fire selector to 3-round-burst mode, Bolan flattened himself against the wall to one side of the door. He eased it open a fraction at a time, then threw it wide and went in fast, breaking to the right. The Beretta tracked ahead of him, seeking a target.

There were two of them. The men were dressed in light tan clothing, and each wore a shoulder rig holding a SIG-Sauer P-226. They had been systematically going through Raymond's belongings, throwing them to the floor once they had finished with them. As Bolan burst into the room the pair turned, hands reaching for the holstered autopistols.

"Leave them!" Bolan warned.

The Beretta was already on line, the muzzle unwavering as it covered the pair.

One decided there was no point in trying to outgun a pointed weapon. He held his hands clear of his body, palms outward.

The other took the opposite path. The why and the how of it never got answered. The gunner had figured he was quicker and possibly never gave his own mortality a moment's thought. It was a costly, fatal mistake, and the guy found that out as Bolan's 93-R chugged its trio of 9 mm parabellum slugs. They drilled into his chest, driving him back across the room. His legs went out from under him and he was dropped to the floor in an uncoordinated heap, limbs jerking in the graceless twitch of approaching death.

Bolan aimed the muzzle of the Beretta at the survivor, leaving him in no doubt as to the seriousness of his position.

"Any more of you around?"

The guy shook his head. "There was only Stoller and me."

"Ease the gun out with your left hand," Bolan instructed.

The man did as he was told.

"Toss it on the couch, then move to the side wall."

Once the man was clear, Bolan picked up the SIG. He ejected the magazine, working the slide to lose the chambered round. He returned the empty gun to the floor.

"Question and answer time," the Executioner growled.

The man shook his head. "No way. I might be out of the game, but I'm no grass."

The man's use of British slang and his accent gave his nationality away. There was something in his manner that also identified him as ex-military. It was the way he carried himself and in the tone of his voice.

"Maybe I'll just turn you over to the local law," Bolan said. "I'm sure they'll be happy to get their hands on someone involved with the killing of one of their people."

"Don't know what you're talkin' about, chum. I don't see any body. Except Stoller's. And *you* killed him."

"Maybe you want to join him."

The Briton shrugged. "I knew when I got in this game I'd die sooner or later."

"Don't feed me that. Nobody wants to die sooner than he needs to."

The man shrugged restlessly. His eyes never once drifted from Bolan's face, and it was that uncompromising stare that caused something to click in the Executioner's mind.

He moved a split second before the slim-bladed knife slid into the man's hand from the sheath strapped to his forearm under his shirtsleeve. In a continuation of the shrug, the guy flicked the knife across the room at Bolan. The Executioner dived to the left but failed to get completely clear, and the blade sliced the flesh of his right side, just above his ribs. He felt the burn of cold steel, followed by the rush of blood from the gash.

Bolan's right hand maintained its grip on the Beretta. He fired on the move, sending a 3-round burst at the knife thrower, his intention to wound rather than to kill. The guy twisted off balance as two of the 9 mm slugs chewed at his left side. He stumbled over a chair, crashing facedown on the floor.

Three long strides took Bolan alongside the downed man. He caught hold of the guy's shirt and flipped him onto his back, ignoring the cries of protest. The warrior was in no mood to be sympathetic. He'd been shot at, taken a fall over a cliff and been left for dead in the sea. He had also witnessed the cold-blooded killing of a courageous young police officer. Bolan figured it was time for answers, and he wasn't worried how he got them.

Bunching his fist in the loose cloth of the guy's shirtfront, Bolan hauled him bodily across the room and dropped him into a chair. He jammed the muzzle of the 93-R against the man's cheek.

"No more stalling, friend," Bolan snapped. "You give me the answers I need and do it fast."

"If I don't?"

"I've got enough reason to pull the trigger on you right now," Bolan said. "All I have to do is remember the way you killed Lisa Raymond."

"Give me a break," the man grumbled. "Look at me. I'm bleeding all over the place. If I don't get medical help, I'll be dead anyway."

"Just keep remembering that while you're refusing to help me."

The Briton stared into Bolan's graveyard eyes and recognized the shadow of death in their icy depths.

"Telling you won't help. You can't get to the people involved. They'll cut you down before you're close. Hell, man, these people aren't bloody playacting. They're damned serious. And they have contacts on the island."

"Like Robert Johnson?" Bolan asked suddenly, throwing in the name Lisa had given him.

The Briton's reaction was enough to convince Bolan that Lisa had been right. Whomever Johnson was, he was known to the wounded man.

"So you know about Johnson. Big deal. You'll still get yourself blitzed if you try anything."

"My worry," Bolan said.

He fished the now-crumpled envelope from his inside pocket. Pulling out the damp photographs,

Sloan's legacy, he thrust one under the wounded man's nose.

"Who are they?"

The guy stared at the images, his own included, in front of him.

"You had the bloody things all the time."

"And you wasted your time trashing the place. Now give."

"What's to tell? We work for the cartel. Covert hit team. All ex-military. Mostly Yanks, but there was me and Cabot. We both did time in the SAS. You killed Cabot outside. The redheaded feller. Most of us have done work for the Colombians already—training their people, setting up camps. Now we're based here in Jamaica to handle problems. We're to eliminate anyone who causes any upset around the Caribbean and on the U.S. mainland."

"Who in particular?"

The man shrugged, then grimaced at the pain it caused.

"Whoever we get the word on. Judges. Lawyers. Top cops. Federal people. DEA."

He was part of an assassination team, plain and simple, set up by the Colombians with their usual efficiency and ruthlessness: see a problem, eliminate it.

"Still ain't going to help you, mate," the wounded merc whispered, and exploded into action even as he spoke.

His abrupt recovery almost caught Bolan unprepared. He began to pull back from the savage assault, angry at allowing the other guy to take him by surprise.

The attacker's lunge out of the chair drove him bodily against the Executioner, one hand reaching for the Beretta, fingers clamping over the barrel and forcing it toward the ceiling. A stunning elbow smash clouted Bolan across the side of the head, breaking his concentration for a few seconds. The Briton followed up with a hard knee that slammed into Bolan's hip. The blow had been aimed at the Executioner's stomach, but his agile retreat allowed him to avoid that. Even so he was driven off balance by the attack. He felt himself being driven back across the room, under a relentless barrage of blows. The merc had been trained in the school of dirty fighting, and he used every trick he knew in a desperate attempt at gaining the advantage over his foe.

The assault might have overwhelmed any other man, but Bolan was a warrior who had dedicated his very existence to combating the forces of evil in every form. That everlasting war had taught him many things, one being the art of survival, regardless of the situation.

Bolan put that philosophy into action, responding to the other man's violence, and feigned a moment of weakness, allowing his resistance to lapse. The move fooled the merc and he changed his stance in the hope of delivering a final blow to Bolan.

The Executioner sensed his opponent's momentary hesitation and used it to make his own assault. He drove his fist into the Briton's bloody side, directly over the bullet wound. The punch was delivered without mercy and drew a moan of agony. Bolan rapped a solid right against the side of his adversary's jaw, snapping his head around.

The warrior felt his gun hand slip free from the merc's grip. He twisted his body, bringing his right leg up in a powerful kick that terminated against the guy's upper chest, driving him back across the room, arms flailing wildly as he struggled to maintain his balance. He failed. Catching his heel against the leg of an armchair, he went over backward, the base of his skull slamming into the corner of a low, solid-wood coffee table. He hit the floor hard, his body arching in reaction to the savage bite of pain, then he dropped flat.

Bolan slumped to his knees, tension draining from his aching body. He remained in that position for a long minute, drawing in slow, deep breaths. It felt as if every inch of his body were alive with pain. He would feel warm fingers of blood streaming down his face from cuts and gashes. The left side of his mouth had already begun to swell.

When his breathing had resumed its normal pace, Bolan climbed to his feet and put away the Beretta. Crossing to where the merc lay, he checked him over. The guy was dead. Bolan went through his pockets and relieved him of his personal belongings. They failed to yield much information. There was a substantial sheaf of bank notes in the guy's wallet. Bolan took the money. He was going to need it. His own cash stake had been lost in the grenade attack at his hotel. The only other items of use were a spare clip of 9 mm ammunition for the man's handgun and a car key on a leather tag. Bolan repeated the search on the other dead merc. The result was the same, netting him little more than another sheaf of bank notes and two more clips of ammo.

Searching the room, the Executioner picked up the weapons the dead men had been carrying. He tucked one of the P-226s in his belt, and retrieving his scattered photographs, went to the bathroom. He stripped to the waist and spent the next few minutes cleaning himself up. Peering in the mirror over the basin, he studied his battered face. In a few hours he was going to look a mess. He stopped the bleeding from the cuts, then dried himself. Pulling his shirt and jacket back on, he returned to the living room and went outside to check the car the two mercs had concealed in the trees near the house.

The car was a new Ford four-door sedan. The sticker on the windshield told Bolan it was a rental. He climbed in and started the engine. Reversing out of the trees, he rolled the car onto the track that led to the road and turned in the direction of Ocho Rios.

Bolan had no definite plan of action for the moment. His priority was to find a place where he could rest and tend his wounds, while at the same time formulating his battle plan. Up until now he had been on the defensive, pushed and chased by an enemy who had managed to remain in the shadows. That was about to change. The Executioner was switching to combat mode. The enemy might not have been aware of it, but Mack Bolan had put them on borrowed time.

Jamaica was about to experience a Bolan blitz.

8

Ocho Rios turned out to be a straggle of hotels, shops, houses and fast-food restaurants. The tourist town gave the appearance of having been laid out along the coast with little thought to anything other than convenience. When the Caribbean cruise ships tied up in Ocho Rios Bay, they brought visitors and money.

Mack Bolan discovered that two of the great cruise liners had docked at Reynolds Wharf, which lay opposite the bauxite terminal. He couldn't fail to notice the red dust from the bauxite that lay over the area.

He had driven along the coast road, checking out the area, searching for a place to park. He needed to pick up some dark clothing for the campaign that lay ahead.

The arrival of the cruise ships meant Ocho Rios was flooded with tourists. Bolan decided this could work in his favor. The streets were going to be crowded, the shops busy. With luck he'd be able to make his purchases and leave without arousing too much interest.

He parked the Ford in a street close to the Coconut Cove Shopping Center and traveled the rest of the way on foot. He located a clothing store, and it took him no longer than ten minutes to find what he wanted: a black turtleneck sweater and slacks, and a black zippered windbreaker. On his way out of the store he spotted a street seller hawking sunglasses. Bolan bought a pair, then merged with the other shoppers.

Returning to his car, Bolan eased back into the traffic on the main drag, jostling for position along with the taxis and minivans. He looked for a telephone and drew alongside the first booth he spotted. Picking up the receiver, he called the operator and asked for the number of Cross Brothers. He memorized the number and broke the connection, then dialed the company. The woman who answered was only too eager to help.

"My company has recently decided to establish a branch in Jamaica," Bolan said. "We handle heavy machinery, and I've been asked to set up a meeting with your Mr. Johnson. Now, this might seem lax on my part, but I don't believe I have his company title in my notes. Could you let me have it so I can put it on the letter I have to send him?"

"No problem. Mr. Johnson is the company distribution manager, but I think you have the wrong man. You need to talk with Mr. Cunningham. He's the plant and machinery manager."

"Seems I have to thank you. Someone in my office hasn't done their homework," Bolan said. "Well, I'll be in touch with Mr. Cunningham. Thanks again."

Bolan made another call. This time to Stony Man and Hal Brognola. When the big Fed came on the line Bolan said, "Call me back on this number."

Brognola took the number and hung up. Moments later the phone rang.

"Go ahead, Striker."

"I'll make this quick. The mission has gone to hell. Sloan is dead. So is his local contact and the cop who was working with Sloan. This is deeper than we thought. The Colombians have set up some kind of hit squad and based them here. This squad's going to take out individuals who get in the traffickers' way. I'm talking about the U.S. mainland. I'm trying to pick up on these people, but right now I'm working cold."

"No help from the local law?"

"I haven't asked and I won't," Bolan replied. "The feeling is there could be an inside man, so I can't take the chance."

"Looks like I've handed you a bad deal, Striker," Brognola said. Bolan caught the apologetic tone.

"It's the way the cards fall. Nobody's fault."

"Anything you need?"

"All my equipment and finances have been lost. The trouble is, I don't have time to wait for a drop. But I do need you to run a check on a name for me. Robert Johnson, distribution manager for the Cross Brothers company here on the island. They're in the bauxite mining business. I need to know everything you can get on this guy."

"Will do," Brognola promised. "Give me a couple of hours."

"I'll call," Bolan said, and hung up.

Back in the Ford the Executioner cranked up the engine and moved on. He had a couple of hours to kill before talking to Brognola again. He drove west out of town, picking up the signs for Dunn's River Falls. The falls were a local attraction. Wooded limestone cliffs, situated in a large park, gave birth to a number of waterfalls that splashed and cascaded down the misty slopes. In the park were snack bars and souvenir stalls. Bolan parked the Ford among the other vehicles in the lot and wandered around aimlessly, appreciating for the brief time at his disposal the natural beauty of the area. He found a quiet spot, sat with his back against a tree and took out the envelope Sloan had given him.

He studied each photograph carefully. Although Sloan had been unable to put names to any of the faces, he had noted the location of each shot. It was obvious that the majority had been taken by long-distance lenses.

A group of three photographs showed a number of people in conversation on a dock. Behind them was a long line of warehouses, and on the extreme left of the shot was the stern of a large oceangoing ship. It was only after checking the photographs for the second time that Bolan identified one of the men in the group.

He knew the face well.

It belonged to one of the mercs he had been forced to kill at Lisa's bungalow. The one named Stoller.

There was another familiar face, black this time, and belonging to the leader of the trio Bolan had faced outside Winston Rogers's place.

He was making connections, vague and insubstantial to anyone except himself. As far as Bolan was concerned the connections were solid. He was picking up the strings. He needed the substance to draw them all together now.

Maybe Robert Johnson would provide it.

AT THE END of the two-hour deadline, Bolan had located another pay phone on the fringes of the park. He got through to Stony Man, and as before, had Brognola call him back. The big Fed's voice was slightly distorted and echoing due to the scrambler system.

"Your friend Johnson has an interesting history," the Justice man reported. "American father and Canadian mother. Well educated, but prone to living above his means. If it comes down to calling it as it is, Johnson is a wheeler-dealer. The guy has been involved in a number of shady deals, but he always seems to walk away clean. The Bear did some sleight of hand with his computers and ran down some bank accounts Johnson has in the Bahamas. It seems he's spreading his assets. And there are some big amounts that have no connection with his job at Cross Brothers."

"Payoff money?"

"The guy's paying for an expensive apartment in Nassau. He also runs a sixty-foot ocean cruiser he moors in Montego Bay. Apparently he lives on board. The boat is called the *Cayman Queen*."

"Could be a good place for me to start," Bolan said. "Have you found anything to connect Johnson with the Colombians?"

"Nothing definite. We do have some copies of photographs from Jack LeGault, Sloan's boss. A quick check has given us a couple of names. One is Rio Santos, a cartel member from Medellín. Another interesting character is Brett Hornaday. Ex-CIA turned mercenary. Known to have worked for the Colombians. He's bad news, Striker. The man has no scruples. He has a regular bunch under his command, a mix of American and British mercs. We're still trying to pin some names to other faces. If you have the opportunity, check in again and I'll update."

"If I have time. Thanks for the names. Sloan passed me copies of the photographs just before he was killed. I may be on the move from here on in. It's hit-and-git time, so you'll hear from me when the situation allows."

"Take it easy, pal," Brognola said.

"Don't I always?" Bolan asked, and ended the conversation.

Early evening found the Executioner in Montego Bay, wearing the dark clothing he had purchased in Ocho Rios. The Beretta nestled in its holster beneath his left armpit, and the SIG-Sauer was tucked under his belt at the small of his back. Bolan would have preferred something heavier. A 9 mm Uzi would have been handy, but he accepted he was going to have to work with the weapons he had until he could lay his hands on something else.

The Ford rental was parked in a quiet back street, which would allow Bolan a fast getaway from the town.

The warrior had done a recon earlier in the day, checking on the cruisers anchored in the blue waters of Montego Bay. The *Cayman Queen* was moored some distance from the quayside. Bolan took note that there were a couple of casually dressed men on board who were plainly on sentry duty. He watched the cruiser for another hour and was rewarded when two men—both black—were rowed out from the quay and boarded the vessel. One of the figures was easily recognizable. It was the Jamaican thug he had met outside Winston Rogers's apartment building. A short while later a car drew up on the quay and disgorged four people. They were hard-faced and expensively dressed, and the Executioner knew who they were the moment he set eyes on them.

Colombians.

They climbed into a waiting motor launch and were ferried out to the cruiser. As they climbed the gangway, they were met and welcomed by a tall figure dressed in a tan suit.

There was something going down that Bolan wanted to know about.

He checked out the quay, which was lined with a multitude of small boats. There had to be a place where he could hire one. He asked a couple of the locals and was directed to a lanky Jamaican squatting beside a couple of small rowboats. Within a few minutes Bolan had a boat in the water. He fixed his oars and rowed out across the placid waters of the bay, keeping his eyes on the *Cayman Queen* as he eased by other vessels moored in the area.

The sun was sliding below the horizon, laying an orange glow over the land and sea. Shadows lengthened, spreading across the bay, helping to conceal Bolan's progress as he closed in on the cruiser. Lights shone from the ship's portholes.

Bolan approached the vessel from the stern. He took the rowboat in beneath the overhang created by the cruiser's aft deck, securing it by a rope to one of the stern lights. He shipped his oars, placing them carefully along the bottom of the boat. By standing erect and stretching at arm's length, Bolan was able to get a grip on the stern rail and pulled himself on board. He remained hanging for long seconds while he checked that the patrolling sentries were amidships. Once he had confirmed the coast was clear, albeit temporarily, he slipped over the rail and crouched in the shadows offered by a raised deck hatch.

From his hiding place the warrior was able to assess the obstacles he might need to overcome. It appeared that the only people on deck were the two sentries. But that situation could change very quickly. The Executioner knew that any incursion into enemy territory was odds on against the perpetrator. The enemy was on home ground and had no reason to conceal himself or worry about betraying his presence. That was the problem of the intruder. If he wished to carry out his probe without being discovered, he had to be on his guard for the complete time he was in enemy territory. None of this was new to Bolan. He had carried out such exercises countless times, and he knew the drill. He also knew, from experience, that there were never any guarantees. Soft probes, by their very nature, were liable to go hard at a moment's notice. Once that happened it became necessary for the intruder to withdraw, and withdraw quickly.

Bolan picked up a sound. He peered around the edge of the hatch and spotted one of the sentries moving along the deck in his direction. He saw now that the man was armed. He carried a Heckler & Koch

MP-5 K submachine gun. The model was the ultra-short version, easily concealed, though the sentry had loaded his with a 30-round magazine.

The sentry moved toward the stern with an easy gait. The subgun swung at his side from a shoulder strap. Something in the way he moved told Bolan he wasn't going to stop short of the stern. And that meant he was going to walk right by the Executioner's place of concealment. Unless the guy was blind or dead drunk, there was no way he would fail to spot Bolan.

He positioned himself for a fast strike, and would need to time it well—in the moment the sentry rounded the hatch but before the man had time to register the shape of the intruder.

Luck took a hand in the proceedings. Instead of turning directly at the hatch, the sentry continued straight on and leaned both hands on the stern rail as he stared out across the twilight of the bay. Bolan breathed a quick prayer to whichever spirit had decreed the guy should take a moment's pause, then rose dark and silent from the shadows. He reached the sentry in two swift strides, reaching around to clamp one big hand over the H&K and secure it. His right hand spread against the back of the sentry's skull. Powered by all the strength in Bolan's arm, the hand shoved down hard, keeping up the pressure until the guy's forehead slammed against the hardwood of the stern rail with a heavy crunch. The sentry stiffened, his body curving, then his legs gave and he flopped in a loose sprawl. He would have pitched over the rail if

Bolan hadn't held him back. Lowering the guy to the deck, the Executioner relieved him of the subgun. A swift search located another clip in the guy's back pocket. Bolan took hold of the unconscious man's belt and dragged him along the deck until he was able to roll him out of sight beneath a rack that held spare sails.

Slinging the MP-5 K from his shoulder, Bolan moved along the deck at a steady stroll, imitating the sentry's walk as best he could. Moments later he saw the other sentry approaching. Bolan studied the section he was in, noticing a walkway between two deck structures. As the second sentry closed the gap, the warrior tensed, preparing himself for the confrontation.

It came faster than he had expected. Light from a porthole fell across Bolan's face, illuminating it in front of the sentry's eyes. In an instant the man reacted, going for his subgun.

The Executioner didn't hesitate. He lunged forward, looping a hard right fist that connected with the guard's jaw. The heavy punch snapped the guy's head around, blood spraying from torn lips. He stumbled, off balance, forgetting the weapon he carried. Bolan gave him little opportunity to recover. He followed his first punch with a second, putting every ounce of his considerable strength into the blow. It drove the sentry up against the side of the deck structure with enough force to drive the air from his lungs. As the man's legs began to give way, Bolan caught him and dragged him into the walkway. Unbuckling the guy's belt, he used it to secure the man's wrists behind his back. He searched the unconscious guard, finding another spare clip for the H&K, and a switchblade in a back pocket. A wide strip of cloth cut from the guy's shirt proved to be an effective gag. Bolan slipped the closed knife into his pocket, then took the loaded magazine from the man's subgun.

Creeping along the deck, Bolan eventually located the main cabin. It was partially below deck, with the upper section jutting some five feet above. The warrior crouched by one of the small portholes and peered through. Below him he could make out the luxurious cabin area. It was well equipped with chairs and a large table. There was even a bar at one end.

The Colombian and the Jamaican heavies were there, as well as three men Bolan recognized from Ed Sloan's photographs.

One of them was the hard-eyed man Bolan had taken special note of, and standing closely behind him was his Oriental bodyguard.

The guy who had welcomed everyone on board was behind the bar, mixing and handing out drinks.

Bolan felt certain this was Robert Johnson.

The group seemed to be enjoying a period of socializing, talking among themselves, mingling. They all appeared to be at ease in one another's company.

The warrior watched with a feeling of mounting irritation. He could see but he couldn't hear what was going on. He needed to be closer, or at least in a position where he might pick up the conversation. From his position he glanced at the ceiling of the cabin. It was fitted with a number of skylights, and he saw that two of them were open to allow fresh air to circulate. Easing away from the porthole, Bolan moved around the cabin until he located a short metal ladder that allowed him access to the cabin roof. He moved across it light-footed until he was able to crouch beside one of the open skylights. Even before he settled in position he was able to hear the voices from the cabin below.

"Gentlemen, I believe it is time we got on with the evening's business. Can we take our places at the table?"

There was a general murmur of assent.

Peering over the rim of the skylight, Bolan saw that he was positioned just slightly off center over the table. He watched the group circle, then settle at the table. Only the Colombian speaker remained standing.

"Good," he said. "Welcome, my friends. I hope that tonight's meeting will be frank and open, and we will be able to clear up a few grievances."

The Colombian sat down.

"I think the first thing we need to discuss is this person we have running all over the damn island," the hard-eyed man said bluntly.

"Yes, I agree," the Colombian said. He glanced across at the speaker. "You did tell me you would take care of him, Brett."

"Yes, man, you said we couldn't handle it," one of the Jamaicans said. "Give it to you and watch how it's done. That's what you promised."

"And I will," Hornaday replied, smarting under the Colombian's unwavering gaze. "Cabot took the assignment, but, to put it bluntly, he fucked up. Simple as that. He lost a number of his people and ended up dead himself. I'm making no excuses, Rio. We failed. But we won't fail again."

"I hope not," the Colombian, Santos, said. "You all know the importance of this operation. Jamaica could be a very profitable venture for us all if we manage our affairs thoroughly. What we do not need, especially at the outset, is interference from the U.S. administration. Also, Brett, we are depending on your team to provide us with a way of striking back against the Americans when they seek to put us out of business. Let us not forget the great deal of money and effort that has been expended in order to establish you and your people here on the island. Medellín will be expecting results."

"You'll get them," Hornaday promised.

Santos nodded. "First I wish to conclude the details of the next shipment to the U.S. Is everything in order, Robert?"

The man Bolan had tagged as Robert Johnson leaned forward across the table.

"All set to go," he confirmed. "The consignment will be loaded on the ship tomorrow afternoon, just before the bauxite is put in the hold. The ship leaves for the States early the following morning."

"You will supervise this yourself?"

"Yes, sir," Johnson replied. "My people at the dock are all ready. I'll be there to oversee the loading."

"Make sure you are," Hornaday said tersely. "We don't want anyone nosing around and asking questions."

Johnson rounded on the merc. "You just provide the muscle, Hornaday. I'll hold up my end. Let's not forget my part of the deal has worked fine. The storage warehouse. A boat to carry the shipment. Even the base you're using up in the mountains. Don't call my arrangements, Hornaday, when security is going all to hell because one guy is chopping you hotshots to pieces."

Hornaday had half risen from his seat when Santos waved him back.

"He does have a point, Brett. A lesson for us all to heed. Let's make certain everything goes smoothly tomorrow."

The merc slumped back in his seat, looking eyes with Johnson.

"My people will be there," he said.

Johnson smiled. "Then we're all safe, aren't we?" he said dryly. "Drink, anyone?"

Santos pulled a long, thick cigar from a silver case on the table in front of him. He lighted the cigar and blew a thick wreath of smoke from his lips.

"If all goes well, the consignment will bring us more than twenty-five million dollars from the American buyers. The schedule calls for two shipments a month. A good way to recoup the losses the cartel sustained from the American strike at Medellín."

"Has there been any information forthcoming on who was responsible?" Johnson asked.

The Colombian seated next to Santos shook his head. "We have no definite information on them. It has to be admitted that they were very professional and very thorough. Our thoughts are they were some covert American strike force."

"Which is why we have formed our own group," Santos explained. "To return to the Americans the kind of treatment they meted out to us. If they want war, then war is what they will get. Only this time it will be fought on their own soil. I will be interested to see how they react to having their precious United States of America invaded."

"You mentioned earlier that our first target has been identified," Hornaday said. "Can we hear who it is?"

Santos nodded. He snapped his fingers and one of his people slid a brown folder across the polished table. The Colombian picked it up and pulled out a photograph.

"This man is Jack LeGault. He is a section chief in the DEA. The agent we eliminated, Sloan, was under his direct orders. LeGault is an important member of the DEA, an experienced narcotics agent who possesses much knowledge and practical dealings with drug-related matters.''

Santos handed the photograph to Hornaday. The merc studied it with interest.

''In this file is all the documented information we have on LeGault. We have also found out that he will be visiting Nassau in two days' time. I do not want him to leave there alive, Brett. He must return to the States in a body bag.''

Hornaday smiled. ''Guaranteed.''

On the roof of the cabin Mack Bolan silently countered the merc's claim with a promise of his own. As long as he had the power to prevent such an occurrence, he would. The only thing that could stop him would be his own death, and the Executioner had no intention of allowing that to happen, either.

About to return his attention to the conversation below, Bolan heard a man yell a warning from somewhere on the cruiser's deck. There was no need to wonder why. The reason was patently obvious.

The Executioner's penetration of the cruiser's defenses had been discovered.

Bolan moved away from the skylight. He had to exit the vessel in the shortest time possible. It would be only a matter of moments before the occupants of the cabin came rushing up on deck. As much as he wanted to engage the enemy, Bolan knew he had to choose his place and time. The cruiser offered neither. It might turn into a floating death trap as far as he was concerned. It wasn't worth taking the chance to find out.

On his feet Bolan slung the H&K across his back by its strap and made sure the extra magazines were secure. With a quick glance at the distant quayside, he ran for the edge of the cabin roof, gathering momentum as he moved. When he reached the edge he launched himself in a full-length dive, clearing the side of the cruiser and cleaving the placid waters of the bay.

The dive took him well below the surface, his powerful strokes propelling him through the warm water. He remained submerged for as long as he could, only surfacing when the need for air became urgent. He broke the surface gently, only feet away from the sleek hull of an anchored motor launch. Bolan trod water and watched the activity on the *Cayman Queen.* He could imagine the frustration of those on board as they scanned the waters of the bay. Their thoughts would be murderous, but within the confines of the bay, surrounded by other boats and so close to shore, there was nothing they could do.

Easing away from the protection of the motor launch, the Executioner swam in the general direction of the quayside, searching for a quiet spot where he could get back onto dry land without arousing any suspicion. He moved from boat to boat, using them for cover. Eventually he pulled himself out of the bay in a quiet corner of the harbor. He stayed concealed in the shadows until the surplus water had drained from his clothing. He closed the windbreaker, zipping it up to conceal the H&K and the holstered Beretta. Keeping to the darker shadows, Bolan made the return journey to where he had left his car.

He approached the side street cautiously. As he rounded the end of a building he stopped short, catching sight of an armed uniformed figure stepping out from the darkness. Bolan recognized the uniform of the Jamaican police. The car was under surveillance, and no longer of any use to the Executioner.

Bolan doubled back, walking slowly, not wanting to arouse suspicion. He cut through a cross alley that brought him to a busier thoroughfare. He merged with the crowd, losing himself within its jostling ranks.

10

By midmorning the following day Bolan was watching the entrance to the dockside facility of Cross Brothers Limited. The business owned its own shipping and freight division. As well as the mining, Cross Brothers handled other kinds of freight, which meant a busy stream of vehicles in and out of the dock area.

Bolan had returned to Ocho Rios during the early morning, taking a local bus. He had spent the night in a cheap hotel in Montego Bay, after picking up from a local market a sturdy carryall that would hold his weapons. The room he'd rented had provided him with the basics, which was enough for Bolan. He needed rest and got it, sleeping lightly with his Beretta in his hand.

At first light he had checked out, grabbing coffee and a sandwich from a stall at the bus depot. He let himself fall in with the line of people waiting for the bus that would take them to Ocho Rios. The coach was old and dusty. Bolan found himself a window seat before the surging crowd filled the interior. The ride was long and slow, interrupted by numerous stops along the way. There didn't appear to be any regular stops. The driver halted the coach when people wanted to get on or off. It was a noisy, jostling ride, with the passengers talking nonstop. Others played loud music. Young children laughed or cried, according to their mood.

Bolan closed his mind to the overwhelming cacophony and concentrated on his plan of action once he arrived in Ocho Rios.

There was no one he could trust. He was totally on his own, with hostile elements out to terminate him on sight. With their contact in the Jamaican police, the enemy also had a good ally. Bolan's on-island activities were, in the eyes of the law, completely unsanctioned. He was operating outside the law once again. The situation wasn't new to Bolan, nor did it bother him to a great degree. But it was something he could have done without.

His prime objective was to eliminate the Colombians, their drug-trafficking operation and the hit squad they had organized. Once he reached Ocho Rios he was going to have to contact Brognola and pass along the information regarding the intended hit on Jack LeGault. After that he would concentrate on removing the Colombians from the Jamaican scene.

There was only one way to handle the drug traffickers and their hirelings—an all-out blitz, striking deep and hard into the heart of their operation. From experience Bolan knew that the Colombians adhered to a single-minded philosophy where business was concerned. They chose their area of operation, moved in and set up shop regardless of social or moral considerations. Anyone who stood in their way had two options: accept a buy-off or be wiped out. Clean and surgically neat. The drug barons had little time for indecisiveness. You were for them or you were against them.

Bolan's hands-on experience of the Colombian drug machine accepted the principle of their doctrine—and he responded in similar fashion, using his own strict code of ultimate justice.

His first strike would be against the drug-shipping operation. In order to carry that through he needed to get inside the dock area and locate the drug cache.

On his arrival in Ocho Rios Bolan located a pay phone and put through a call to Stony Man Farm. When Brognola came on the line the Executioner gave him the rundown on the planned assassination attempt on LeGault.

"I don't know how or when," Bolan concluded. "If I get to these people in time, I might be able to put them out of business before they start. If not, just make sure LeGault is made aware of the strike."

"I'll tell him. The problem is getting him to cancel his visit. LeGault is a stubborn man. Tell him he's walking into danger and he'll go right ahead and do it. Kind of like someone else I know. By the way, how's it going out there?"

"It's lean-and-mean time," Bolan told him, explaining his position. "It keeps me on my toes. I'll call you when I can."

Bolan was understating the situation. He was well aware of the odds. The enemy would be on their guard following his penetration of Johnson's cruiser. It would be a natural assumption on their part to connect the intruder with Bolan. And that connection would pose the question—how much had Bolan overheard? The response would be to put their people on full alert, especially around the dock area. Protecting the drug shipment due to leave Jamaica would be priority.

Bolan's strike at the Colombian drug setup needed to be hard, deep-cutting, and capable of inflicting as much psychological harm as possible.

Part of his intention was to unsettle the cartel. They had established a base in Jamaica with their usual confidence, believing that ruthless efficiency and dollar power was all they needed. Harsh action against anyone attempting to interfere with the Colombian business organization was intended to have a twofold effect. As well as removing the threat posed by Ed Sloan and his partners, the deaths would be used as a warning to anyone else considering resistance.

That might have been the intent. As a warning to deter Mack Bolan, the killings had the opposite effect. He wasn't so naive as to believe that sudden death was only visited on the guilty. In the ongoing war against evil there were casualties on both sides. That was inevitable. No one was invincible. The distinction lay with the motivation.

The Colombians had engineered the deaths simply because there was a direct threat to the security of their illegal business dealings. They viewed it as a means to protecting their interests, which in Bolan's mind was a chilling excuse for ending three human lives.

Mack Bolan's kills were determined by the necessity to cut away the cancer that was eating away at the fabric of civilized life. The individuals who came into his sights were the unrepentant destroyers of life and normality. The Executioner had taken it upon himself to eliminate the lawbreakers, the killers, the betrayers, and his instant justice reclaimed some of the damages owed to the innocent. It wasn't a perfect solution, by any means, but until someone came along with a real answer, Mack Bolan was willing and determined to carry on with his war.

Right now Bolan's objective was to get inside the dock area. The main gate was flanked on both sides by high steel fences running parallel with the road. The warrior considered going in from the ocean, then abandoned the idea just as quickly. It would take too much arranging, especially as he was going to have to carry it out during daylight.

He was watching the traffic moving in and out of the gates. Regular appearances of high refrigerated containers, pulled by diesel tractors, gave him food for thought. He wandered back along the street, looking for an opportunity to put into action the scheme he had in mind.

Bolan crossed the road, cutting across to a section where road repairs had caused a temporary traffic jam. He slipped around the far side of the snarled-up vehicles, crouching as he passed the blockage. He had noticed one of the refrigerated trucks in the line and walked alongside the forty-foot container, out of sight of prying eyes.

Bolan crouched beneath the chassis and scanned the undercarriage of steel cross beams. Jamming the carryall between two struts, he pulled himself up off the road, hooking arms and legs around cross sections. He pressed himself against the aluminum base of the container seconds before air brakes hissed and the rig jolted into movement.

The next few minutes passed in noisy discomfort. Bolan hung on to the chassis sections, his body aching from the effort. The noise beneath the moving rig was deafening, the hot air full of dust and fumes. The rigid construction of the chassis shook him around without letup. Each time the massive wheels of the rig dropped into a pothole, Bolan felt as if his arms were being wrenched from their sockets.

The rocking motion of the rig slowed, then ceased Bolan peered around and caught a partial glimpse of the fence flanking the gates to the dock. He saw the uniformed legs of the security man as he stepped out of his gatehouse to talk to the driver of the rig. After what seemed an eternity the rig lurched forward, through the gates and into the dock complex. The vehicle rolled along the dock area, making a number of

turns before it rolled to a stop outside a large refrigerated warehouse. The tractor fell silent as the driver
cut the power. He climbed down from the rig and
vanished inside the warehouse.

Bolan released his grip, lowered himself to the
ground and retrieved the carryall. Crouched beside the
rear wheels, he surveyed the area. It was temporarily
deserted. The warrior emerged from beneath the
chassis and ducked out of sight behind the generator
unit that provided power for the refrigerated warehouse.

He was inside the dock complex, but he needed to
locate the drug cache. It wasn't going to be easy, unless he obtained some help. The only man on the dock
who could help him was Robert Johnson. The man
was supposed to be around to check on the consignment. And the consignment was going to be loaded on
one of the company ore-carrying ships.

Keeping to the rear of buildings and using all the
cover he could, Bolan worked his way deeper into the
complex. He took the time to conceal himself behind
a stack of timber so that he could hang the H&K
subgun beneath his black windbreaker. The SIG-Sauer
was tucked under his belt in the small of his back. He
had taped together the spare magazines for the H&K,
and these were inside the jacket's inner pockets along
with extra clips for his two pistols. He would have
preferred his combat harness and blacksuit, but they
were somewhere in the Caribbean. He stowed the
empty bag out of sight beneath the timber stack.

Before he became too involved in the mechanics of the operation, Bolan decided to do a recon. He wanted some idea of the number of hardmen waiting for him to show. He also needed to familiarize himself with the layout of the area and pinpoint avenues of escape in case he found himself wanting a fast exit.

He spotted a number of forklifts parked beside a battery-charging terminal. A hard hat and clipboard rested on the seat of one of the trucks. Bolan took a casual walk past the vehicle, lifting the clipboard and hard hat. When he emerged on the main walkway of the complex, he was wearing the hat and checking items off from the clipboard as he strolled in the direction of the main dock quays, which lay at the far side of the area. He portrayed the attitude of someone who knew exactly what he was doing and who would stand no nonsense from anyone interfering. The workers he passed as he made his way through the complex eyed him and remained at a distance. He was challenged only once, by a guy who had just climbed down from an overhead crane.

"Hey, what you doin' lookin' at my machine, man?" the burly Jamaican asked.

Bolan glanced at him sharply. "I'm doing my job, friend. Checking this place for the insurance company. If there's no insurance, you don't get compensation in the event of an accident."

The Jamaican considered the statement.

"That right? Guess so. So how we doin'?"

"Fine, as far as I can see. Hey, maybe you can help me. I need to talk to some guy called Johnson. You know where I can find him?"

The crane operator nodded. "He'll be down at the end quays." He pointed into the distance. "Mind, you'll be lucky to see him, man. They got some important cargo goin' out today so the gates are closed down there. Pretty damn hard to get in that place unless you have clearance."

"I have to try," Bolan said. "Thanks for your help, friend."

The Jamaican raised a big hand as he walked off, leaving Bolan to continue toward the secure area.

Important cargo, the Jamaican had said. Bolan smiled grimly. If he had his way that important cargo was going to be permanently impounded.

11

"Quit pacing up and down," Brett Hornaday snapped.

Robert Johnson threw a scornful glance in the mercenary's direction.

"What do you want me to do instead? Open a bottle of champagne to celebrate this whole deal going down the tubes?"

"Forget last night," Hornaday suggested. "Let's deal with today."

"With that guy running around loose? He probably knows too much about our business already. I just forget him?"

"If he shows up here, we'll handle it."

"Haven't I heard you say that before? I wish I had your confidence."

"If you were a professional, you would have."

"Excuse me if I don't share that sentiment," Johnson replied. "You and your *professionals* haven't exactly done too well up to now."

"Meaning?"

"Meaning that this single guy has run rings around you. He's walked away from every encounter, notching up kills each time, and last night he even breached the security you set up on my boat and listened in on our meeting. I might be a civilian in these matters, but in my book that adds up to egg on your face."

Hornaday turned away from the office window, from where he had been looking out across the quayside. The merc's face was taut with rage. He confronted Johnson.

"I wish we didn't have to deal with people like you," he said evenly. "But we do because you have something we need. You couldn't wait to take up the offer Santos promised you. The trouble is you have no commitment. All you see is the money. Nothing else. The first problem that comes along, you wet yourself and start thinking about pulling out. No chance, pal. You are, as they say, in for the duration. This is no one-off bribe. When you sign on with the cartel it's for good.

"Now I'm not denying we've had problems with this guy. But I don't surrender the war because I've lost a couple of skirmishes. I've learned from them. I understand this guy, the way he behaves. It's told me a lot about him. He's like me. He's no cop. Not DEA, either. I'd say he's a soldier, a guy who knows his way around a battlefield. Because believe me, Johnson, we're in a goddamn war, right up to our ears."

"If he's not a cop, then who the hell is he?"

"A specialist," Hornaday replied. "A guy who decided a long time ago that he had to handle things his own way."

Spendloe, who had been listening and watching, turned his attention on Hornaday. There was a bright gleam in the man's eyes.

"Sweet Jesus," he murmured softly. "Do we have the same guy in mind, Brett?"

"Think about it," the merc said. "The MO fits. Who else could have taken on Cabot and the crew when they hit that cop's place? Even with a chopper along for backup."

"Mack Bolan!" Spendloe breathed. "I thought he was dead."

Hornaday smiled. "So did a lot of people. Until his style of operating started to show up again a couple of years back."

"Who are you talking about?" Johnson asked.

"Mack Bolan," Spendloe said. "The guy they tagged the Executioner. Waged a one-man war against the Mafia some years back."

Johnson's face registered the shock that hit him.

"You mean you believe this Bolan is the one who's been targeting us?"

"I think so," Hornaday said.

"My God, if he's on our tail, we might as well quit right now."

"He's only as good as you allow him to be," Hornaday said. "The man isn't indestructible. He can be killed. He can be stopped. The guy is good. You'll get no argument from me on that one. But I won't let that stop me doing what I'm good at myself. If I'm correct and we are up against this guy, Bolan, then his long run is going to come to an abrupt end."

Johnson held the merc's gaze. He wasn't as convinced as Hornaday seemed to be. The more he recalled about the man named Bolan, the faster his resolve weakened. Hornaday and Spendloe, all wrapped up in their macho images, scared him just as much as the Executioner. And he was right in the middle of it all. When the bullets started flying—and he was certain they would—he was going to be right there on the firing line. He knew that for a fact. And he also knew that there was no way of avoiding involvement. Whichever way he turned, all the doors marked Exit would close in his face.

This was one situation he couldn't buy his way out of.

The more he thought about it, the more likely it seemed it was going to help to bury him.

12

The final section of the dock complex was, as the Jamaican crane operator had said, fenced-off from the main area. A high, steel, chain-link fence stretched from the water's edge, back across the dock frontage. Behind the fence were three large storage warehouses. Berthed against the quay was a large bulk-carrier ship, its paintwork stained from constant exposure to the reddish ore-bearing bauxite that it carried.

Maintaining his role as insurance assessor, Bolan had worked his way along the dock frontage, giving himself time to observe the access point to the restricted area. There was no chance of his getting in through the gates. A gatehouse was constantly manned by two Jamaican heavies in uniform.

Bolan's examination of the fence told him that he was going to have to find another way in.

Still some distance from the restricted area, he turned and worked his way to the rear of the complex, keeping the distant fence parallel with his line of travel. Minutes later he stopped at the extreme limit of the complex. The high outer fence he had seen from the road presented him with a virtually unscalable barrier. The warrior's only entry to the restricted area was the lower but solid chain-link fence. He studied it from his place of concealment behind some rusting machinery, which included a couple of ancient mobile cranes.

The task appeared hopeless at first. The fence was of heavy construction and heavy-duty cutters would be needed to open a hole. The base was set below ground level to prevent entry from that angle.

The Executioner's gaze was drawn to one of the abandoned cranes. The machine's jib, extended and with its cable and hook still in place, rested near the fence. Bolan studied the dangling steel cable, following an imaginary line over the top edge of the fence to the flat roof of a building that stood no more than ten feet from the fence. Then an idea formed in his fertile mind.

Bolan crossed to the abandoned crane. He got rid of the hard hat and clipboard, and without a moment's hesitation climbed up on the crane, working his way to the extended jib. He hoisted himself on top of the steel structure and crouch-walked his way along the angled extension. By the time he reached halfway along the jib he was more than thirty feet above the ground. From this position he was able to look out across the intervening space to the flat-roofed building. It looked a great deal farther from his high elevation than it had from the ground. Bolan calculated the extent of the swing he might achieve via the crane cable. It would be close, and he would get one chance to make it work. If he gauged his swing correctly, the curve would place him just over the edge of the flat roof at a height of around five to six feet.

It was only as he looked out across the expanse of the flat roof that he saw the helicopter resting on the landing pad painted on the surface. There was something familiar about the aircraft. Bolan recognized it as the helicopter that had backed the hit team at Lisa Raymond's house.

Climbing higher up the jib, the warrior caught hold of the dangling cable and drew it to him. He retraced his steps back down the jib, pulling the cable with him. The steel hook at the end of the cable was small enough for him to grasp with both hands. Bolan checked the area around the crane and saw no workers in this rear section.

He gripped the hook, edged to the side of the jib and balanced precariously while he prepared himself. Leaning out as far as he could, Bolan allowed his body weight to drag him clear of the jib. He felt his arms and shoulders take his full body weight, the muscles groaning in protest. But there was no going back. He was already swinging out from the crane, the air rushing by his face, the distant building suddenly beginning to loom large in his eyes.

He reached the lowest point in his swing, clearing the top of the chain-link fence. Then the arc of his pendulum began to rise. He saw the concrete face of the building rushing at him and for a chill moment it seemed he was going to smash into it headfirst. Almost as if it were melting in front of him, the wall slid away. Bolan cleared the edge, his swing taking him up and over the roof. He felt his forward motion slow rapidly, realizing he needed to let go or the cable would drag him back. He released his grip, relaxing his muscles as he dropped. The roof's surface sped up to meet him. His feet struck and Bolan went with the force of gravity, knees bending, rolling forward. The force of his landing stunned him briefly as he slithered across the rough surface, arms thrown up to protect his head.

Bolan pushed to his feet instantly, ignoring the aches and pains burning his battered flesh. He needed cover in case his unorthodox means of arrival had been observed. His right hand pulled down the windbreaker's zipper and pulled the Beretta 93-R. The autopistol was already set for 3-round bursts.

He had almost reached the cover provided by the helicopter when he caught the sound of footsteps on the rough surface of the roof. Peering around the tail rotor, he spotted a pair of anxious Jamaicans, both armed with 9 mm Uzi machine pistols. They had appeared from a metal staircase that allowed access to the roof.

One of the men was busy arguing with his partner, insisting that he had heard something. He confirmed it when he spotted the still-swinging crane cable.

"I told you some son of a bitch was up here!" he repeated. "There!"

Bolan leaned out from the helicopter's fuselage and stroked the trigger of the 93-R. The Beretta coughed tightly, expending its triple shots. The Jamaican caught the slugs in his chest. He whirled, a startled expression on his face, then crumpled onto the roof, arms flung wide.

The second guy floundered, searching the area for the unseen gunman. His hesitation gave Bolan the edge he needed. He touched the 93-R's trigger a second time. The 9 mm rounds pounded into the guy's skull, misting the air red around the shattered head. He went down hard, and stayed down.

By the time Bolan reached him he was as dead as his partner. He relieved the bodies of their autoweapons, slinging the Uzis from his shoulder, noting that each weapon had double magazines, one taped to the other, for extended firepower.

Before he left the roof the warrior checked out the helicopter. Repair patches on the underside of the fuselage confirmed that it was the machine he had shot at. He checked the cabin, flicking switches to make sure the craft was ready to fly. It was. Bolan was no Jack Grimaldi, but he had enough expertise to get a chopper into the air and take it to where he wanted to go. If he had the opportunity to get back to the helicopter after his strike, it could provide him with a means of a clean getaway.

Bolan moved quickly to the staircase and took the steps down two at a time. He reached ground level without being seen, or seeing anyone himself. There was ample cover for him to use as he moved toward the quayside.

His need now was to locate the warehouse containing the drug cache. And when he did locate it he would have to destroy it. That would hurt the Colombians more than anything else. The Executioner's intention was to hit the drug traffickers where it hurt most—in their wallets.

Studying the rear walls of the three warehouses, Bolan noticed that the end building had an armed man positioned at the small access door. The guy was slim and dark-haired, his clothing expensive and stylish. There was no mistaking his identity. Bolan was looking at one of the Colombian soldiers. He was also, he realized, looking at the warehouse holding the drug cache as it waited to be loaded onto the ore carrier.

The Executioner made his way to the last warehouse unobserved. As the guard stood silently smoking a cigarette, Bolan crept up behind him and snaked a solid muscular arm around his neck, cutting off his wind. The Colombian fought fiercely, but the warrior's superior strength won out. The guard slumped to the ground, unconscious.

Bolan flattened against the wall, then reached out to edge the door open. He peered around the frame, making sure there was no one immediately inside before slipping across the threshold, dropping into a combat crouch, the 93-R up and ready.

Hazy sunlight showed at the far end of the long building, where the warehouse doors stood wide open. Bolan could see men moving near the entrance. At his end of the warehouse there was little natural light. The only illumination came from skylights set in the high roof, and those were coated with the grime of years, barely allowing sunlight to penetrate. The light that did come through pierced the gloom as thin shafts filled with dancing dust motes. There was enough for Bolan to see that the warehouse was stacked with goods of all shapes and sizes. Barrels and boxes, crates and sacks, all were stacked in haphazard fashion, filling the expanse of floor space.

The conglomeration of goods provided the Executioner with ample cover as he threaded his way through, wanting to reach the front of the warehouse in as short a time as possible. He was aware of the numbers counting down. He had to locate and destroy the drug cache, then make his escape.

Concealed behind a final barrier of stacked crates, Bolan surveyed the scene and made his assessment.

Armed men loitered around the warehouse doors. They were a mixed bunch—Jamaicans, Colombians and a number of white faces. Bolan recognized some of them. He had seen them in Ed Sloan's photographs, and also on board Robert Johnson's cruiser. The cast members of Bolan's grim company were becoming familiar to him.

To his left was an office, and he could see a number of men behind the dusty glass windows. Parked close by the office was an open-backed 4×4 truck, its bed occupied by a bulky shape covered by a large canvas sheet. Three armed men were stationed by the truck, and they never once moved away from the vehicle. Their dedication was impressive, and drew Bolan's undivided attention.

The warrior heard a soft scraping sound behind him, very close. Too close. Before he could move, the cold muzzle of a gun was jammed against the back of his neck.

"Go ahead, sucker, just give me an excuse to use this!"

The falling numbers hit zero.

13

Mack Bolan's anger was directed at himself. He had allowed his concentration to wander for a fraction of a second, and during that fragment of time the enemy had located and surprised him. It was the kind of mistake that might easily end in tragedy. But the warrior's anger was short-lived. He accepted his error and responded to it.

The man behind Bolan tapped him on the shoulder.

"Lay the gun down, pal, then stand up slowly."

Bolan obeyed. He placed the Beretta on the floor, tensing his leg muscles as he pushed upright. He felt the muzzle of the gun slip away from the back of his neck as the unseen assailant adjusted to the Executioner's moving form. He had already formed an image of the guy's position from the touch of the hand on his shoulder, and, knowing that he only had scant moments to act, Bolan exploded into movement.

He ducked and turned, bringing his right arm around in a sweep that struck his adversary's gun hand. The blow forced the weapon off target.

The negative side of the action came a split second later when the handgun fired, the gunman's finger jerking against the trigger. The bullet went up through the warehouse roof, out of harm's way. But the damage had still been done. The loud report alerted every man in the warehouse.

Following through, Bolan rammed his left fist into the gunner's jaw. The hard, uncompromising blow broke the man's jaw and loosened several teeth. As the man stumbled away, Bolan bent and snatched up the Beretta. He angled the weapon from floor level, triggering two quick shots that ended the gunman's agony in a stunning burst of pain.

The warrior slid the Beretta back into its holster and brought one of his acquired Uzis into action, working the bolt as he spotted a number of the armed men bearing down on his position.

He waited until their initial rush brought them well within the Uzi's range, then cut loose with a murderous volley that dropped one guy and scattered the others.

A number of autoweapons returned fire, a hail of slugs hammering into the crates that had concealed Bolan. The ammo was wasted. The Executioner had changed position the moment he opened fire. Now, yards to the left of his former position, he emptied the machine pistol's clip in a sustained burst. One trafficker went down, clutching a shattered leg. A second man dropped his weapon as 9 mm slugs tore into his upper chest and shoulder, spilling his blood and his resolve to fight onto the dirty floor of the warehouse.

There was momentary panic as the defenders of the warehouse and its illicit cargo tried to come to some kind of cohesive action. During that time Mack Bolan added terror to their lives. His Uzi, reloaded with its second magazine, opened up again. Slugs burned across the warehouse floor, picking up the retreating figure of a lean, slight Colombian. The drug dealer was attempting to avoid Bolan's deadly fire and clear the jammed breech of his mat-black Ingram MAC-10. He failed on both counts. The subgun remained jammed and the Colombian died as a spray of 9 mm slugs stitched a bloody line up his body from waist to throat.

When the clip was exhausted Bolan tossed it aside and brought the second Uzi into play. He turned his attention on the office, aware of the frantic movement behind the glass. A door burst open and a tall Jamaican, wearing a bright, patterned shirt ran out. He was cradling a Franchi SPAS-12 combat shotgun, the black barrel weaving back and forth as he sought a target. He was blown back through the door with a scything figure eight, the 9 mm bullets shredding his shirt and the flesh beneath. The Jamaican flung out one arm, his fist smashing through the door's glass panel.

Bolan laid down a long volley that shattered the windows the length of the office. The men inside flung themselves to the floor to avoid the bullets and jagged shards.

The noise of an engine bursting into life reached Bolan's ears above the crackle of autofire. He saw exhaust smoke gushing from the truck's pipe as it was wildly revved. One of the vehicle's attendants had scrambled into the driver's seat and was attempting to move the cargo to safety. The other pair of gunners had jumped into the back and were braced either side of the canvas-covered cocaine.

Bolan turned the Uzi on them. His sustained volley cut across both gunmen, ripping into their exposed bodies and throwing them over the side of the truck. Slugs tore into the canvas cover, and white powder spouted into the air.

Racing to the side of the warehouse, keeping stacked crates between himself and the regrouping traffickers, the Executioner fed the second of the taped magazines into the Uzi, cocking the weapon and turning it on the pickup as it accelerated for the open door of the warehouse. Parabellum rounds blasted out the window of the cab, seeking the body of the driver. The guy jerked awkwardly as a half dozen of the slugs drilled into his body. He lost control of the vehicle as it burst through the door and shot across the open quayside.

The lumbering shape of a heavy diesel tractor, hauling a high-sided open trailer, loomed large. The rig was carrying the first load of ore destined for the waiting ship. The driver, startled by the eruption of gunfire, was further surprised when the pickup appeared, heading directly for his rig. In the seconds he had to spare, the driver took the only evasive action open to him. He kicked open his door and jumped from the slow-moving vehicle, and maintaining his balance, ran for his life.

The pickup slewed in a half circle, slamming up against the stalling tractor. The impact was hard enough to burst the tractor's fuel tank, spilling diesel across the hood of the pickup. The liquid seeped beneath the hood and came in contact with shorting wires. The sparks were all that was needed to ignite the fuel. The initial burst of flame fed back across the hood of the pickup and raced for the bulk of the tractor's fuel. The ruptured tank, spraying diesel to the ground as well as over the pickup, added to the growing fire.

Bolan tracked the Uzi on a figure racing across the warehouse. The guy, moving fast, triggered a short burst from a Heckler & Koch autoweapon. He was yelling orders over his shoulder, desperately trying to gather a force behind him to cut off the Executioner's avenue of escape through the warehouse door. Ignoring the steam of bullets hammering the steel drums he was standing behind, Bolan locked on to his target, held, then touched the trigger. The Uzi burst into life, firing a wedge of 9 mm rounds that caught the running man full in the chest. He twisted in agony, crashing hard onto the warehouse floor. His subgun flew from nerveless fingers, clattering across the dirty concrete. The badly hit merc struggled to climb to his feet, dragging an autopistol from a hip holster beneath his jacket. Bolan hit him with a second burst, which drove him over onto his back.

There was a brief, tense break in the firefight.

The warrior took full advantage of the lull. He discarded the almost-exhausted Uzi and pulled his own H&K into play. From his crouching position behind the stacked drums, he surveyed the scene. A number of bodies littered the floor. Some lay deathly still; others moved or crawled, nursing their wounds. Figures in the bullet-ravaged office were moving into view, weapons raised.

As Bolan assessed the situation, his nostrils picked up the sharp smell of pungent liquid. He also became aware of a wet, splashing sound, which he discovered to be liquid spilling from the drums he was using for cover. Jagged bullet holes peppered a number of the drums, and the liquid was already pooling on the floor, spreading out toward the open doorway. The sharp, breath-catching smell came from industrial solvent, and the material was highly flammable.

Rushing figures caught Bolan's attention. He was being approached from a number of directions. The opposition had taken time to organize, and now they were moving in for the kill.

On the quayside the burning pickup vanished in a flashing ball of flame as its gas tank exploded. Burning fuel was thrown in all directions, sizzling across the quayside with fiery fingers. The pickup, engulfed in

flame, lifted off the ground and turned onto its side.
The canvas cover had been dislodged, exposing the
pile of heavy black rubber bags beneath. The bags had
contained kilos of pure cocaine destined for the ore
carrier. Now the drug was overwhelmed by the
scorching heat of the flames, consumed.

Burning debris rained to the ground. Chunks of
scorched metal, flaming plastic and rubber bounced
off the concrete, some landing inside the warehouse
door. One section reached as far as the gathering pool
of solvent.

The solvent ignited instantly, the vapor from the
liquid catching fire with a hungry whoosh. The rising
glare of flame traced its way back toward the steel
drums, leaping across the warehouse floor in a scant
few seconds.

Bolan saw the fire racing in his direction. He pulled
back from the drums, seeking cover, taking a headlong dive over a low stack of wooden crates. As he hit
the floor on the far side, he heard angry yells. Moments later the warehouse shook as a number of the
steel drums were torn apart by the explosion of their
contents. A wave of intense heat washed over the
warrior's prone body as the drums became seething
balls of flame.

Scrambling to his feet, Bolan slapped at a spot on
his sleeve where burning solvent had scorched the
material. He glanced to where the stack of drums had
stood. Some were still intact but the majority had

blown apart, throwing their flaming contents across the warehouse.

The Executioner didn't wait to see if any of the traffickers and their helpers were still around. He had achieved, by indirect means, the destruction of the cocaine shipment and had also taken out several members of the organization. It was enough for a beginning.

Bolan knew the battle was far from over.

He turned and retraced his steps to the rear of the warehouse, counting on the confusion of the fire to screen his escape.

He was close to the door when the chatter of an autoweapon cut across the other sounds around him. Bullets whacked into the raw wood of stacked cases. Slivers sprang into the air. Bolan felt something sting his cheek, and he reacted by dropping to the warehouse floor, rolling for cover as more bullets chewed at the space he had just occupied. Over on his back Bolan caught a blurred image of an angry-faced man leaning out from behind a pile of boxes. The Executioner didn't hesitate. He swung around the H&K, angling upward, and touched the trigger. The bullets caught the unwary guy in his upper chest and shoulder, the impact spinning him out from cover, so that Bolan's second burst took him dead center. The trafficker crashed over onto his back, choking on the blood that welled up in his throat.

Bolan gained his feet, pushing on for the distant exit, reversing the H&K's magazine and cocking the weapon as he ran. Behind him he heard distant thumps as more solvent drums exploded. Added to the roar of the detonation came the screams of men caught in the fiery blast.

The sunlit rectangle of the open door beckoned. Bolan was almost on it when he caught sight of a shadow outside. Someone was waiting to one side of the door, a raised subgun in his hands.

The warrior was counting off the numbers in his head as he neared the door. He had no time for a protracted cat-and-mouse game with the waiting gunman. Others would soon be at his back, and he had no desire to become caught in a trap. He accelerated, pushing hard, and burst through the door in a lunging dive that threw him clear. He landed on his left shoulder, twisting his sliding form, feeling the burn of his contact with the concrete. He was already tracking the surprised gunman even as the other man was switching his aim.

The gunman's Uzi fired first, but he had triggered too hastily. The 9 mm slugs gouged the concrete and whined off into empty air.

Bolan's reply was precise and delivered with a calm head controlling a steady hand. The H&K crackled harshly, loosing a burst that took away half the gunman's face and throat in a microsecond of awful agony. The guy was dumped back against the warehouse wall, his weapon slipping from dead fingers. He hit the ground in a bloody heap, already removed from the real world and lost in a new one of darkness and pain.

The Executioner sprinted toward the far building where the helicopter rested. He moved fast, weaving in and out of the obstacles in his way, counting on his slim lead to allow him the advantage of time. That time would be short, not guaranteed in any way. There were always wild cards in any game, the unexpected twists and turns that fate kept well hidden until the last moment.

For once Bolan seemed to have eluded the unexpected. He reached the base of the iron staircase, running up the side of the building without further challenge. Halfway up, glancing over his shoulder, he saw armed men converging on the building, and knew that his moment of freedom was about to be canceled.

His thought was confirmed when distant autoweapons opened up. Bullets clanged off the staircase, chipping the brickwork around him.

The helicopter, so close a moment ago, suddenly seemed a thousand miles away.

14

Without breaking his stride Bolan turned and emptied the H&K's magazine in the direction of his pursuers. The burst of gunfire scattered the hardmen, granting the warrior the seconds he needed to reach the top of the staircase. He cleared the parapet and sprinted across the roof in the direction of the helicopter.

He yanked open the door and settled in the pilot's seat, flicking switches and pressing the button that fed power to the chopper's engine. It began to turn, with the usual wheezing slowness that was characteristic of helicopters, then caught after long seconds, the power building gradually.

Bolan, anticipating the appearance of the enemy, turned to check the parapet where the curving top rail of the iron staircase showed.

When the first head and shoulders became visible, Bolan poured on the power, risking everything in a rapid takeoff. He felt the helicopter vibrate as he worked the controls. The craft lifted, then settled, lifting again as he wrestled with the heavy stick. He felt the chopper tilt and swing in a ponderous arc, and for a moment he was sure the machine would slither over the edge of the roof and plunge to the distant ground.

Then he realized the roof was dropping away with increasing swiftness. He fed more power to the engine, balancing the controls with hands and feet, and felt the aircraft respond.

Below him the Executioner saw armed figures spilling over the parapet, spreading out across the roof. The hardmen raised their weapons and fired, the muzzle-flashes winking up at him. He couldn't hear the shots, but felt the impact as a number of bullets hit the helicopter.

He was gaining altitude rapidly now and set the chopper on a southerly course. He wanted to put distance between himself and Ocho Rios.

Just before the chopper took him away from the dock complex, Bolan managed a final overview. He saw the rising plume of dark smoke spreading across the sky from the burning warehouse. Then it slid sideways from his field of vision and was gone.

His probe into enemy territory had inflicted physical damage to the traffickers, resulting in the destruction of the illicit cocaine cache. The Colombians and their associates would be counting the cost to their Jamaican enterprise. It would be in the balance whether they folded their tents and left, or dug in and rebuilt. Bolan knew the Colombians well enough to understand their philosophy when it came to being attacked. Violence had a way of begetting violence. The traffickers were hard, ruthless and unforgiving.

They wouldn't back off lightly. Bolan had inflicted damage, but he had not killed the beast. He'd merely wounded it. And any hunter worth his salt knew that a wounded beast was often deadlier than a whole one.

A clipboard holding a pilot's chart lay on the seat beside him. Bolan picked it up. The chart illustrated the coastal area around Ocho Rios and the Jamaican country to the south and east. The area known as the Blue Mountains lay in the eastern section. Studying the chart, he picked up a penciled-in route from the port to somewhere in the mountain region. He recalled Ed Sloan saying the Colombian base was in the Blue Mountains. The more he studied the chart, the more likely it seemed to offer him a destination. It was his only option for the moment.

Bolan set his course for the remote mountain country island. His intention was to put the chopper down somewhere far enough away from the opposition to enable him to assess his situation and plan his next move, which would be against the base Sloan had identified, where the Colombians' strike force was located. Sloan had talked of an armed, isolated base. Bolan needed to hit it hard and fast, before any significant resistance could be mounted against him.

He had been flying for almost half an hour when he noticed a darkening in the sky to the north. Heavy clouds were forming out at sea, moving inland swiftly. The warrior didn't like the look of the changing weather. The Caribbean wasn't all sunlight and blue seas. The area had a reputation for rapid climatic changes. Torrential rain and high winds were as much a part of the Caribbean legend as was the high, bright sun. The last thing Bolan needed was a tropical storm.

Unfortunately that was what he got.

Within ten minutes of his spotting the dark clouds, the storm had caught up with him. The rain enveloped the helicopter, followed by a strong wind that buffeted the aircraft. Bolan wrestled with the controls, struggling to keep the chopper on a steady course.

The misty peaks of the Blue Mountain range became lost in the downpour. Bolan was forced to keep checking the helicopter's compass in order to maintain his course. His intention was to fly in as close as he could to the mountain base without being spotted. The remainder of the journey would have to be made on foot. That presented no problems for the warrior. His Vietnam experience had taught him the hard lessons where infiltration was concerned. The skills he'd learned there had never left him. They were ingrained, part of him.

The storm increased its intensity. The driven rain lashed out of the gray sky, and the chopper's wipers struggled to keep the Plexiglas clear. Bolan hunched forward in his seat, straining against the safety harness as he peered through the mist. He found he was having to work hard to keep the helicopter on an even keel. The wind that accompanied the rain persisted in its attack.

A long half hour passed. Bolan, struggling to keep the helicopter on course, felt the strain. His arm and leg muscles ached from the constant work at the controls. He fought the desire to relax, knowing that any lack of concentration could be fatal.

He made one of his frequent instrument checks. This time he noticed a drop in oil pressure. Even as he watched, the needle on the gauge dropped again, making a slow, steady fall. The first thing that came into Bolan's mind was the thud of bullets striking the helicopter during its takeoff. Had damage been inflicted that was now starting to affect the chopper's performance?

A break in the weather ahead revealed the green-covered mountain slopes. Bolan became aware of a changing tone to the sound of the chopper's engine. He checked the instruments again and realized he was losing power. The engine faltered slightly, then picked up as he laid on more power. He knew he was only putting off the evil moment. The engine had developed a fault and was edging toward failure. When it did, Bolan was going to be in a precarious position if he maintained his present height.

His decision made, the Executioner began to lose altitude, watching the green carpet rise to meet him. He leveled out just above tree height, cutting back on the power and coasting the chopper in. His eyes scanned the ground below, searching for a clearing where he could land. Minutes passed and he had failed to find anything. The mountain slope below seemed to be covered by an unbroken swath of green.

Without warning, the engine began to run ragged, and power loss was swift. The helicopter dropped like a stone, Bolan wrestling with the controls. The engine caught again, roaring wildly until Bolan got it under control. He brought the chopper back on a level run. He knew his luck was running out. There was no way of knowing how long the engine would maintain its present condition. Failure could occur again in an instant.

His only choice was to put the chopper down as quickly as possible. He had no time left to search for the ideal landing ground. He had to put down immediately.

Cinching his safety harness tight, Bolan worked the controls and felt the chopper sink. Blurred by the rain, the treetops flashed below, so dense that it seemed as though he could land on the very tops of the trees and find them solid enough to support him. The illusion was shattered when the chopper's landing gear ripped through the green canopy. He felt the machine jerk sideways and hung on to the controls with grim determination.

The chopper's engine cut out at that precise moment. It maintained forward motion for a few seconds before gravity took over. The aircraft tilted forward, the cabin sinking through the treetops with a rising crescendo of splintering wood and rustling foliage. The whirling rotors chopped away at the greenery until they snagged and buckled. The helicopter's deadweight took it down through the trees, turning it in a dizzying spiral. All Bolan could do was hang on to the redundant controls, his stomach churning with the ferocity of his descent.

A cracking noise tore through the cabin, and a moment later the passenger door was ripped off its hinges. A chill wind filled the cabin, rain lashing at Bolan. Abruptly the helicopter stopped its downward flight. Bolan was thrown against the safety harness, the straps biting into his flesh and the air pounded from his lungs. He hung, suspended, momentarily helpless. Before he could move he heard a long, drawn-out creaking sound, followed by a loud crack. The helicopter slid sideways, seeming to plunge into eternal emptiness. Something hit the canopy in front of his eyes. The Plexiglas cracked, long spiderwebs distorting his vision. It made the fall worse, like being in a closed, falling elevator. The warrior was thrown back and forth, swung about on his harness. His bruised body cried out for an end to the horrendous ride.

When it came, Bolan was totally unprepared. The descent stopped with a hard, stunning jolt, and he was thrown forward. It felt as if the safety harness were ripping through his flesh, tearing his limbs from their sockets. Pressure built up in his chest and he found it hard to breathe. A second shock followed, banging him about with ruthless intensity. The shock receded. Silence dropped over Bolan; darkness followed swiftly.

15

Rio Santos hadn't said a word during the drive back to the mountain base. He sat in the rear of the black Mercedes sedan, his face impassive, his eyes fixed on the distant horizon. The expression in those eyes was as bleak as the misty rain sweeping across the landscape.

Sitting across from the Colombian, Brett Hornaday was experiencing a degree of discomfort. For the first time in his professional life the merc had been made to look like a fool. He had decided to keep his own counsel on the matter, because he knew that anything he did say would only add insult to injury. There were no two ways about it. Hornaday and his people had been well and truly outclassed. The attack by the man who had breached the restricted dock area had torn them apart.

The invader had gone through them as if he was on a country walk. Not only had he outgunned Hornaday's troops, the guy had also destroyed the cocaine shipment that was due to go to the States. Hornaday knew without asking that Santos felt more loss over the coke than he did over the dead or wounded men.

It had taken a great deal of planning to get the cache—one of the largest the cartel had pushed to the island—in place for loading onto the ore carrier. All the planning had been for nothing. It was also going to cost Santos a great deal of cash to keep the mess in the family. His contact in the local police department was going to have to be well greased in order for him to suppress the incident on the docks. There would have to be a cooling-off period before it would be safe to start the operation up again.

In the meantime Santos needed to show the cartel in Medellín that he wasn't allowing the setback to affect him. That would necessitate coming up with a new way of smuggling the drugs into the States. Not impossible, just irritating.

As far as Santos was concerned, his standing within the cartel would have sunk to an all-time low. His family connection wouldn't make much difference now. In fact it could go badly for his uncle. The man had vouched for Santos, helped to set him up with the Jamaican operation. To lose face with the cartel wasn't a healthy thing to do.

On a personal level, what really angered Hornaday was the nerve of the guy taking the helicopter. It angered him, but it also increased his respect for the bastard. He had balls, he'd give him that much. Not only had he decimated the team on the dock, he had stolen their chopper. That took guts and a cool head. Hornaday wanted to meet the guy. If only to be there when he died. Because such a man would only become safe with a bullet through his head.

Santos suddenly swiveled in his seat, fixing his gaze on Hornaday.

"Perhaps my best move would be to hire this man and get rid of all of you."

His tone was almost light, and it might have been easy to believe the Colombian was joking. Hornaday knew better. He had worked with Santos for long enough to know one thing for certain. That a sense of humor was something the trafficker didn't possess. The man was cold like a fish. Calculating, cruel and totally devoid of any lightness in his personality.

"We haven't made a good start," Santos went on. "I'm sure you agree."

"What do you expect me to say, Rio? I do agree. This whole affair has been disastrous. I've no excuses. I won't blame it on the people around me. I'm in charge, so the failure is mine. All I can say is I don't intend to take this lying down. No bastard does this to me and my group and walks."

Santos allowed a thin smile to mar the marble contours of his face.

"Brave words, Brett, and what I would expect from someone like you. I see only one way to redeem ourselves in this matter. We have to find this man and destroy him. Medellín will be watching and judging us. If we allow this man to get away with what he's done, then the world will not be large enough to hide us. You know the cartel as well as I do. They will not forgive failure."

From his position beside the driver, Spendloe joined in the conversation.

"My guess is this guy is going for the base. Something tells me he won't be satisfied until he's wiped out the whole damn setup."

"My sentiments exactly," Santos agreed. "And the helicopter gives him the best opportunity to reach the house ahead of us."

"Maybe," Hornaday muttered. He reached for the radiophone fitted in the passenger compartment. He sat impatiently until his call was answered. "Carson? What took you so long? We're on the way back. Keep your eyes open for the chopper. It's in unfriendly hands." Hornaday paused as Carson relayed a piece of information. He began to relax, leaning back in the leather seat, a wry smile edging his lips. "Get us many of our people out as you can spare. Make sweeps to cover the area. Carson, I want this son of a bitch alive if possible. But watch him. He's no beginner. He knows his job."

Jamming the handset back on its rest, Hornaday glanced at Santos.

"This might not be all bad," he said. "Carson just told me they've picked up the chopper's emergency beacon signal. It must have gone down. Carson has a fix on it. If our boy is alive and moving, Carson will box him in. I told him to send our people out to track this bastard down. If we can grab him alive, maybe we can find out who's behind him.''

Santos merely raised an eyebrow. He didn't go much on speculation. He needed solid evidence of a kill to convince him they were on track. Up to now he'd seen very little to interest him.

''Perhaps with a little luck we can contain this situation. Eliminate this man and get back to our business.''

''As soon as I have matters under control I want to get back to the LeGault deal. I need to leave for Nassau as soon as possible. I don't want to have to cancel the hit.''

''Let's hope LeGault hasn't been tipped off,'' Spendloe said from the front seat. ''If he has, you might walk into a stakeout.''

''If he hasn't, we lose a good chance to take him out of the game altogether,'' Hornaday replied. ''I think it's worth the risk.''

Hornaday locked eyes with Spendloe. His second in command offered a smile of encouragement before turning back to stare through the windshield. There wasn't much else going, Hornaday thought. He hoped that Carson got his people organized well. It was important that they catch the man who had been raising so much hell.

Important for the cartel.

For Santos.

But mainly it was important for Hornaday. He wanted the guy badly. So bad he could taste it. The trouble was, it was a bitter taste and Hornaday didn't like that, because it kept reminding him of defeat.

The only consolation was the possibility that the guy *was* Mack Bolan. Now that would be a victory to crow about—Brett Hornaday, the man who engineered the Executioner's demise.

16

The soft, insistent beeping sound broke through the mist of gray fog enveloping Bolan. He moved slowly, testing his limbs in case he'd suffered a break. There was a lot of bruising but no pain from splintered bone or ruptured organs. The Executioner opened his eyes, blinking away the drifting haze. He was staring at the Plexiglas canopy, which was covered with a crazy pattern of cracks. He gazed around the cabin. Everything that was loose had been thrown back and forth. The main instrument panel had been jolted out of position.

Bolan was still strapped into the pilot's seat. The fact he had been secured had probably saved his life.

He could still hear the soft beeping and realized it was an electronic sound. Seconds later it came to him what the sound was—an emergency signal. Automatically set off in the event of a crash landing, the device sent out a signal that could be picked up by the helicopter's base, letting them know that the craft was down. The base had only to lock on to the signal and they had a location for the helicopter. In times of emergency the signal could mean rescue for the pilot and crew of a crashed chopper.

In Bolan's case the signal would bring sudden death at the hands of his rescuers.

The warrior released the safety harness, shrugging out of the webbing straps. His battered body groaned in protest as he moved. He reached to the cabin floor and picked up the Heckler & Koch subgun. Searching the floor, he located the clipboard with its chart. He pulled the chart from the clip and stuffed it inside his jacket. Turning on the seat, he kicked open the pilot's door and eased himself out of the buckled mess of the cabin. The ground lay some four feet below. Bolan dropped to the rain-soaked, spongy earth, and, gaining his feet, he moved swiftly away from the wrecked helicopter.

Crouching in the lee of a rocky hummock, the Executioner hunched his shoulders against the driving rain. From his new position he was able to take in the crash scene. He could see where the falling helicopter had torn its way through the close-knit trees, ripping off branches and scarring trunks. It had come to rest a few feet from the forest floor, wedged between the massive trunks of ancient trees.

Before he did anything else Bolan had a weapons check. The H&K was still his main weapon, and he had a couple of magazines left for that. The Beretta, snug in its holster, had two clips, as did the SIG-Sauer. He would have preferred a stronger complement of weapons, but his situation dictated otherwise. Additional hardware would have to be gained if and when the opportunity presented itself.

He took out the chart and checked his position. The course he'd been flying had to be translated into ground-level topography. Locating the enemy base would be that much harder now. There was a great difference between spotting from the air and plotting his route on foot. Every undulation in the landscape became an obstacle. In the type of mountain country he was traveling, Bolan would find himself having to go around some natural obstacles simply because he wouldn't be able to go through or over them. These restrictions would add time to his trek. It was something the warrior could have done without. The arduous walk would tire him, and that factor had to be taken into account. No fighter could give his best when he was exhausted.

Bolan managed to pinpoint the main peak he had been observing while flying. If he managed to keep that in the same position in relation to his line of travel, he would eventually hit the base. Timewise it would take him a great deal longer. Added to that was the fact that the enemy would be out looking for him. The advantage there was slightly in his favor. They would be out in force, looking for one man. He could hide, putting the onus on them. And if they came searching for him they would be exposing themselves. Bolan's expertise as a marksman would serve him well.

He moved out, traveling at a steady pace. He had no intention of tiring himself by pushing too hard. The skill was in covering distance and also conserving energy. Bolan used the natural terrain of the landscape to conceal his movements. He avoided any high areas where his moving figure could be seen from a distance, even in the rainy conditions. He stayed low, in shadowed areas, blending in with the foliage. He paused often, checking his surroundings and choosing his way ahead before covering the next stretch. That way he was able to make the maximum use of natural cover, while also making certain no one was in the vicinity.

The warrior fell back into this mode with natural ease. The Executioner was home. The forested terrain provided him with his ideal environment. Here he operated as one with the land, he made it his ally, used it to his advantage. And in doing so became invisible to his enemy.

He had been on the move for almost an hour when he picked up the first signs of men moving through the forested slopes. They were spread out in an attempt to draw him into their sweep, but the very fact they were distanced from one another necessitated the use of walkie-talkies. Bolan picked up one of their terse conversations, the speaker passing within feet of the Executioner's place of concealment.

Bolan allowed the man to pass by and end his radio message before he struck from behind, taking the armed hunter out with a single 9 mm bullet from the silenced Beretta. Crouching beside the body, he quickly stripped it of weapons and radio. The man had been wearing a camouflaged flak jacket, which Bolan donned. There was also a keen-edged hunting knife sheathed on the guy's belt. Bolan transferred it to his own. He left the handgun but took the dead man's M-16 assault rifle. There were three spare magazines in the pouches of the flak jacket.

Changing direction, the warrior angled slightly west of his previous line of travel, moving out to intercept other members of the group tracking him. The more he disabled now, the less he'd have to face once he hit the base.

Easing through the undergrowth, Bolan heard the radio on his belt crackle, then a voice came through. He ignored it, wanting the opposition to become aware of a change in their status. He needed them to know the game was altering.

Minutes later Bolan spotted another figure moving along the edge of a stream. The watercourse had been swollen by the downpour. The armed man was speaking into his radio and failed to notice Bolan until it was too late. His eyes, moving restlessly about the forest landscape, picked out the Executioner's figure in the split second before Bolan triggered the 93-R. The guy toppled over backward, a 9 mm slug buried in his skull. He rolled into the stream, the water carrying him away in a swirl of bloody foam.

Holstering the Beretta, Bolan was about to slip back in the shadows when he caught sight of a figure partway up a slope above the stream. The hardman's M-16 was already aimed and tracking. The Executioner dropped to the ground, and as he rolled away from where he'd landed, he heard the M-16 open fire. The wet earth close by erupted as the 5.56 mm bullets ripped into it. The final rounds of the volley were so close that Bolan felt their impacts as they ate into the ground.

The firing ceased as the gunner moved down the slope, hoping to close in on his target.

Bolan, prone on the ground, caught the move and used it to his advantage. Coming up on one knee, he shouldered his M-16, aiming and snapping off two fast shots. The first missed. The second was fired after Bolan readjusted his aim and it caught the gunman in the chest, driving him off his feet and slamming him back against the slope.

Time to head for cover. The shots would draw the others fast, intent on closing the net they had been casting. He had been hoping to pick them off one by one, reducing their numbers while remaining out of sight. The eruption of gunfire made that impossible. The pursuit would heat up now, and his ability to move among them at will had been reduced.

Bark from a nearby tree trunk flew into the air. Bolan ducked below a low branch, pausing in a thick clump of ferns as he considered his next move. The shot had come from ahead of him, which meant that the noose was tightening. They were closing in.

He held his position long enough to pick up the sound of someone heading in his direction. The man was doing little to conceal the sound of his approach.

Confidence was making someone careless. Bolan, back pressed against a thick trunk, waited.

The man burst out of the thick undergrowth, moving quickly, his rifle up and ready. He was moving too fast to read all the signs around him, and failed to spot Bolan's close presence. His awareness came too late. Two bullets from the Executioner's M-16 caught him in the chest, driving into his heart. The guy went down without a sound.

Bolan drew back deeper into the undergrowth, letting the shadows claim him. He remained hidden, his ears attuned to the sounds of the forest.

The first thing he noticed was that the rain had ceased. Water continued to drip from the leaves, but overhead, through the close canopy of treetops, the warrior caught a glimpse of the blue sky.

The end of the storm denied Bolan the cover of the falling rain. He regretted it, but accepted the fact and put it out of his mind. His main concern was staying alive and outwitting the opposition.

A voice from the radio drew his attention. Bolan unclipped the handset and listened in on the cross talk. Unwisely his opponents had chosen to use an open channel, each man conversing with the others at the same time. The Executioner extracted as much information as he could from the babble. From the number of different voices, he calculated there had to be at least five men left alive. Unless there were others not speaking over the open channel.

The Executioner replaced the radio and moved deeper into the forest, making a wide detour. His intention was to fall behind the enemy, becoming the hunter and not the hunted. These men had come tracking him with the intention of either capturing or killing him. Now they were on the Executioner's list, and he wasn't held back by a dependency on others. Bolan, as always, fought a lonely war. Once the lines were drawn he became dedicated to the task ahead, allowing nothing to deter him.

The enemy had laid down the ground rules and had condemned themselves by their actions, the evil business in which they dealt and their ruthless intent to remove any and all opposition.

Mack Bolan moved silently through the forest, homing in on his targets. He closed his mind to everything but the matter that lay before him.

He was well aware that the hardmen remaining at the base would be expecting him if he survived this first encounter. They would be on full alert.

But that knowledge would not deter him. Bolan's long-running war had become almost a continuous campaign, pushed forward by his own momentum. Taking the fight to the enemy was routine as far as the Executioner was concerned. It was his style to carry the war forward, to deny the enemy any respite, preventing as far as was possible the opportunity for them to regroup and strengthen their resolve. Hit them hard and hit them again. It was the only way.

It was Bolan's way.

And he would not—could not—ever change it.

BOLAN STALKED the hunters, silently watching as they searched the area. The only finds they made were the bodies of their partners. Watching and listening from the undergrowth, the warrior picked up the unease that was permeating their ranks. They held hurried discussions over the radios, then, as if by common consent, the individual members of the team came together, merging into one group.

It was the event Bolan had been waiting for. Now he had them all together. Six men, armed but unsure of their safety. Bolan's initial sniping had decimated their power, leaving them in a vulnerable position. Despite still having numerical superiority, the warrior's opponents had lost the edge. His initiative, forcing the pace of the battle, had hurt them physically and psychologically. He had pushed them to the edge, breaking their advantage.

Feeding a fresh magazine into the M-16, Bolan cocked the weapon, then moved in for the kill. He had to catch them before they decided to spread out again.

His first volley cut down two of them where they stood, the semiauto fire pumping a stream of 5.56 mm slugs that ripped the life from them.

Wheeling, even as he ran forward, Bolan cut loose as one guy broke from the main group. The runner was one of the Colombians. He yelled his defiance, swinging around his own M-16, determined to make a fight.

The Executioner drove a trio of slugs into his chest, slamming the trafficker to the sodden ground. The Colombian slithered forward on his face, ungracefully departing the life he had wasted.

Of the remaining three, one stood his ground, wild anger coloring his lean face as he triggered a volley of shots in Bolan's general direction. His aim was close, but close was no good. The warrior dropped to one knee, turning sideways, narrowing his body-line target. He snugged the M-16 to his shoulder, snap-aimed and placed two bullets between the shooter's eyes. The guy curved over backward, then crashed to the ground.

The moment he'd fired at the single man, Bolan rolled forward, sliding into a slight dip he'd sighted. His move took him out of view of the remaining pair. The bullets they had fired in the Executioner's direction only bored into the earth. The target had apparently vanished.

It reappeared seconds later. The muzzle of Bolan's M-16 slid over the lip of the depression, tracking on the pair as they raced across the forest floor in his direction. His first shot hit dead center, tearing through the target's chest and into his heart. The second guy veered to the right, away from Bolan's line of fire. He triggered his own weapon, sending a stream of slugs into the earth just short of Bolan's depression. The damp earth exploded, briefly obliterating the Executioner's view of the area. He pulled back, then wriggled to the far end of the depression, pulling himself to the lip so he could check the area. He caught a fleeting glimpse of the surviving gunman as the guy dived from sight behind a wide tree trunk.

Bolan scrambled to his feet. He wasn't going to let the pace slacken now. He couldn't afford to. One man was all it took to fire the bullet that might end Bolan's career.

He hit the trees, dodging the low branches. The M-16 probed ahead, the muzzle seeking its target. Bolan paused beside a trunk, pressing close for protection, his ears straining to pick up any sound, no matter how slight.

At first there was nothing. Only his own breathing. The warrior steadied himself, still listening, waiting for the slight whisper that would give away his opponent's presence.

The noise was a long time coming. The hardman had played the waiting game before. The guy was sitting it out, too, expecting Bolan to make an error. But the other guy moved first. He was merely changing position, trying to relieve the stiffness in his lower limbs.

Bolan picked up the rustle of clothing. It was off to his right, no more than twenty feet. He peered in that direction, eyes trying to penetrate the shadows in the thickness of the foliage. He caught the faintest gleam of light striking metal.

The Executioner brought the M-16 into play, saturating the position with a sustained burst. He heard a subdued groan as his shots struck their intended target. A figure rose from the undergrowth, still clutching his M-16. The front of the guy's camou shirt was dappled with a spreading bloodstain. He stumbled forward, then abruptly toppled facedown on the damp ground.

Scanning the area, Bolan remained where he was until he had satisfied himself there was no further threat. He eased out of his place of concealment and crossed to check the downed traffickers. None had survived the encounter.

He relieved the dead men of their weaponry, laying it out and choosing what he needed. He took all the spare magazines for the M-16s. One of the mercs had a string of grenades attached to a combat harness. Bolan stripped the harness from the corpse and took a small backpack from another, which contained a few items of canned food. He discarded the food and filled the pack with the spare magazines. Having second thoughts, he opened a couple of the food cans and ate the contents.

Picking up the trail, Bolan headed out. A glance at his watch showed it was late afternoon. He wasn't going to reach the base before nightfall. That suited him. The darkness would be his ally. He could make it work for him and against the enemy.

17

The day was slipping away fast. Shadows were lengthening, pushing out across the landscape, by the time Bolan reached the base. It lay a quarter mile distant, above Bolan and on a plateau surrounded by heavily timbered slopes.

Bolan welcomed the oncoming night. It would cloak his movements, providing him with cover during his assault.

The spacious house had been built for privacy and nestled in the feral greenery of the forest that helped to isolate it. Its location told of the builder's need to be alone, away from people and the trappings of civilization.

A different need for privacy dominated the lives of the new occupants. They desired to be alone because their business kept them apart from their fellow man. Polite society shunned them, afraid of their potential for violence and the evil of their squalid trade. The drug merchants saw only the flood of dollars coming their way, yet they were aware of the stigma attached to the business and held themselves apart.

For all practical purposes the mountain base was the cartel's center of operations for the Caribbean. And in line with the Colombians' keen sense of self-preservation, they had made the house and grounds secure.

Secure meant armed guards, four of them, patrolling the perimeter wall. Bolan had also spotted the powerful floodlights on top of high steel poles.

The Executioner moved in closer, checking every step of the way. He needed to be sure there were no sentries patrolling on his side of the wall. His vigilance paid off. It took some time, but he was eventually satisfied that the Colombians had decided on a purely defensive stance. They were going to protect their base from the inside.

Within a hundred yards of the wall, Bolan was able to study the sentries' patrol routine. It wasn't particularly complex. Each guard handled one side of the compound. The warrior decided to wait until full dark before he went over the wall. Once inside he would deal with the sentries.

As the sun sank out of sight beyond the horizon, the floodlights came on, spearing through the darkness and casting brilliant splashes of illumination across the compound. They were fixed lights, which meant they couldn't be moved to pick up any particular area. And due to their positioning, there were a few poorly lighted spots. One lay only yards from where Bolan now crouched at the base of the perimeter wall. He chose this as his entry point.

His observation of the sentries had given him a rough timetable of their movements. He had calculated that he would have under a minute to get over the wall and take out the guard on this section of the wall before the guy patrolling the adjacent section reached the corner.

Securing the M-16 across his shoulders, the warrior unsheathed his knife and eased into position by the wall. The barrier was only four feet high, so he had little problem getting over the top.

Bolan listened as the sentry tramped by, gave him a count of five, then reached up and hauled himself over the wall. He dropped flat at the base, pressing close to the ground where the light was at its weakest. He held the knife ready in his right hand.

The Executioner could see the dark shape of the sentry as the guy reached the end of his patrol section. He turned and began his return trip, each step bringing him closer to where Bolan lay in wait. The warrior let the man walk past before approaching from behind like a silent shadow. His left hand reached around to clamp over the man's mouth, stifling any outcry. His right thrust forward, the keen blade of the knife piercing clothing then flesh. Bolan shoved hard, driving the knife in deep, then he cut sideways, severing the spinal cord. The stricken sentry arched violently, and Bolan had to clamp his arms tight to restrain him. Then the man collapsed, his limbs losing their strength. The warrior lowered his burden to the ground.

Bolan stayed low, close to the wall, moving quickly so he could be waiting at the corner when the second sentry made his appearance. He was there with seconds to spare.

The sentry, a Jamaican, expressed pure terror when Bolan rose out of the shadows. When he opened his mouth to yell, the warrior lunged forward, the heavy blade of the knife cutting a short, sharp arc across the guy's taut throat. The flesh parted, spilling blood in a rush, and the Jamaican's yell died in a gurgle as he dropped to the ground. Stunned and dying, the sentry lost his battle for life in a spreading pool of glistening wetness.

Sheathing the knife, Bolan armed himself with the M-16. He took aim and shot out first one spotlight, then the other, plunging the front section of the house and grounds into darkness. Swapping the rifle for the Beretta set for 3-round bursts, Bolan headed for the house, sprinting across the dark lawn that surrounded the sprawling house. He would have preferred to carry out a soft probe, so he could have gained some idea of the layout. Time and circumstance had disallowed that. He'd have to hit the place blind, depending on surprise and a degree of luck.

He was halfway across the lawn when sudden, blinding light hit him.

A spotlight on the roof.

Bolan wheeled, changing direction. He dived into the darkness, flat on the lawn, unslinging the M-16 as he heard voices calling from the house. He slammed

the butt to his shoulder, aimed and fired a steady burst
at the spotlight. The light jerked, sweeping back and
forth. Someone began to fire from the rooftop, but the
bullets were way off target. Bolan shifted position and
fired again, triggering rapid shots at the center of the
brilliant ball of light. The spot exploded with star-
tling suddenness. Snatching up the 93-R, and with the
M-16 in his left hand, Bolan broke for the side of the
house.

A figure loomed from the shadows. Bolan triggered a burst, and the guy screamed and fell.

The night exploded with gunfire. Bolan ducked,
rolled, came to his feet yards away. He could hear the
hail of bullets slapping the lawn off to his right. Dead
ahead the warrior made out the shapes of several cars
and trucks—the motor pool. He hit the ground,
crawling close to the vehicles, palmed a grenade and
popped the pin. He tossed the missile back across the
lawn, then crawled around the rear end of a 4×4.

The grenade exploded with a sharp crack. In the
brief glare of light, Bolan saw figures hurled in all directions. Then the warrior was up and running for the
house.

He reached the stone wall, flattening against it. Two
figures burst into view from around the far side of the
house. They opened fire, bullets chipping into the
stonework close to Bolan. Dropping to one knee, the
Executioner leveled the Beretta and fired, the controlled bursts punching bloody holes in the traffick-

ers' chests, scattering bodies across the gravel path in squirming heaps.

Bolan checked out the side of the house for access. There was nothing on this section except for a large picture window. He made his own access by putting a couple of bursts through the glass. The window splintered, glass crashing to the ground and into the room beyond.

Gunfire erupted inside the house, the shadows lightened by the bright muzzle-flashes. Bolan unhooked and armed a grenade, counted down, then tossed it through the window. A heartbeat later an explosion wrecked the room, and as Bolan went toward the window, a bloody, tattered figure stumbled into view. The guy had caught part of the grenade blast. The left side of his face was raw and bloody, and one arm hung loosely at his side. He still carried an autopistol in his good hand. Bolan dropped him with a burst from the 93-R. Leathering the Beretta, the Executioner climbed in through the shattered window, with the M-16 on semiautomatic. He laid a stream of fire across the interior as he entered.

There was no need. The occupants of the smoking, wrecked room were beyond caring. They lay sprawled across the littered floor, reduced to bleeding, scorched corpses. On the far side of the room a door hung at a crazy angle, one hinge torn free. Light from a passage shone through the swirl of smoke.

Bolan paused to one side of the doorway. He checked the remaining grenades on his harness. Of the three left, two were fragmentation, the third concussion. He unclipped the bomb, popped the pin, tossed the missile down the passage, then covered his ears and shut his eyes. The concussion grenade exploded with a stark flash of high-intensity light and a sharp crack. Anyone caught near the blast would suffer perforated eardrums and temporary blindness.

Giving the effects a couple of seconds to wear off, the warrior ducked through the door and walked along the hallway.

One guy was down, pawing at his skull as he tried to make sense out of the silent, unseeing world he had been plunged into. Farther along, two more gunmen, less severely affected, tried to take on the Executioner as he stormed the passage. Bolan's M-16 took them out with a burst of flesh-searing 5.56 mm slugs. The gunmen backpedaled along the hallway, their bodies twitching violently under the impact of the bullets. They stumbled and fell as Bolan charged past them.

He emerged in a low-ceilinged lounge, furnished with expensive leather-bound armchairs and couches. Stereo equipment lined one wall, and in a corner a large-screen TV played to a vanished audience.

The occupants of the room were heading for the wide double-doors on the far side of the room, weapons in their hands, when one of them caught a glimpse of Bolan.

He yelled to his partners, drawing their attention to the intruder. The mixed group of traffickers—Jamaicans and Colombians—reversed their retreat and swung back into the room. They caught the full fury of Bolan's M-16. The volley of shots bounced them against the wall and doors, leaving bloody smears on the white paint and polished wood.

Dumping the empty magazine, Bolan rammed home a fresh one. He skirted the downed traffickers and checked out the area beyond the door.

He had a quick glimpse of a wide reception area an instant before an M-16 opened up, slugs tearing at the doorframe. A long sliver of raw wood caught the right side of Bolan's face, and he felt the instant spill of warm blood trickling down his cheek. He ducked back behind the frame.

The warrior took one of the remaining grenades, primed it and flung the bomb across the reception area. The explosion rattled the walls of the house. In among the yells of confusion, Bolan heard the crash of splintered glass. Ducking low, he charged through the doorway, breaking to the left, hugging the outer wall.

A bloody figure stumbled out of the curling smoke. Bolan punched a pair of 5.56 mm holes into the guy's chest, knocking him off his feet. He half turned to meet the next attack, clubbing the lunging hardman across the jaw with the butt of the M-16. He slammed back against the hard floor, unconscious and out of play.

Bolan checked the area. Nothing moved. The only sounds he picked up were the groans of the wounded traffickers.

He knew, though, that he wasn't alone. There were the armed men on the roof of the house, plus the survivors on the lawn. Bolan fed a fresh 30-round magazine into the M-16 and repeated the procedure with the Beretta. His reloading was a wise move. Even as he returned the 93-R to its holster, he picked up the sound of hurrying footsteps somewhere above him.

Across the reception area a wide stone staircase led to the upper floor. Two armed figures burst into view on the upper landing and started down the stairs, pushing as they surveyed the damage.

They also laid eyes on the dark-clad figure responsible. The lead man triggered a volley of bullets that raked the floor, yards away from Bolan. The Executioner replied with a rapid burst that split the guy's chest, tossing him against the wall. Before the first man had slithered to the floor Bolan shifted his aim and took out the remaining trafficker.

Bolan heard noise from the rear. The men from outside had followed his trail through the house and were closing in for the kill. Priming one of his remaining grenades, the warrior hurled it through the door into the adjoining room. Startled yells were drowned by the thunderous blast of the detonation. Bolan stormed into the room after the explosion, his M-16 completing the grenade's deadly work. He emerged moments later, once again replenishing the M-16's ammunition supply.

He crossed the reception area, heading for the main door. As he neared it, the sound of a revving engine reached his ears. Bolan sprinted forward, out through the door.

A dark-colored 4 × 4 raced around the corner of the house toward Bolan. In the glare of one spotlight centered on the front of the house he caught a glimpse of the occupants.

There were three men. Santos, the Colombian boss of the traffickers; at the wheel the hulking figure of the Korean bodyguard; and in the rear seat, swinging a subgun in Bolan's direction, was Hornaday, the strike team leader.

The 4 × 4 hurtled at Bolan, its engine racing.

The Executioner had to dive out of its path, unable to fire. As he hit the ground he heard the harsh crackle of Hornaday's subgun and felt the thumps of the 9 mm bullets as they raked the gravel around his rolling body. He grunted as something burned a searing path across his shoulder, then came to rest against an ornamental flowerpot. The impact winded him. For long seconds he was unable to do anything except lie still, listening to the sound of the 4 × 4's engine receding into the night.

AFTER DISARMING the wounded traffickers and herding them into one room that he was able to secure, Bolan prowled the house, making a room-to-room search. His investigation unearthed a number of items.

In the base's communications room he located a radio and telephones. There was also a small computer, complete with telephone modem. The monitor screen showed a list of names and locations. Bolan recognized a few of the names as drug dealers based in the U.S.A. It looked as if he had stumbled across the distribution setup the Colombians were going to use once they had the Jamaican network established.

Picking up one of the telephones, Bolan dialed the number he had for Stony Man Farm, waiting while the electronic security system rerouted the call. Finally the call was answered. The voice on the other end was unmistakably Brognola's.

Bolan waived the niceties, giving the big Fed a concise rundown on the events since their last conversation, and bringing him up-to-date with the strike at the cartel's base.

"Geez, Striker, have you left anything standing?"

"No civilians involved," Bolan replied testily. He was getting tired, otherwise Brognola's sarcasm would have elicited a dry chuckle.

"Is the game over?"

"Not yet. The top men got away from me. But only for now. I'll deal with them later. Is the Bear around?"

"Sure." Brognola put out a call. "You got something for him?"

"The computer here has a lot of useful information. It's got a modem. If the Bear can patch in, he might be able to access the system and pull the information."

"He's on his way. Do you need any help?"

"Give me an hour to clear this place, then contact the Jamaican authorities. If they move fast they can bag this bunch and shut down the organization. They'll need medical help for the wounded. And tell them they have a crooked cop somewhere in the system who's been dealing with the Colombians. He might be the one who fingered Lisa Raymond.''

Brognola sighed. ''This is going to take some explaining.''

''That's your area of expertise.''

''Yeah, right. The Bear's here. What's your next move?''

''The mission isn't over until I cancel out Hornaday and Santos.''

''Jack LeGault wouldn't postpone. He'll be in Nassau by tomorrow, late afternoon.''

''That still worries me,'' Bolan replied. ''I'll be in touch.''

Moments later Kurtzman's grumbling tones reached Bolan.

''You know how to connect the modem?'' the Bear asked. ''Or do I need to explain, using very simple words?''

''I'll do my best.'' Bolan chuckled, his mood easing a little.

He put the receiver into its cradle on the modem and keyed in the operating instructions, leaving Kurtzman to delve into the information stored in the computer's memory.

Making his way outside, Bolan checked the parked vehicles. He chose a Mitsubishi 4 × 4 with a full gas tank and keys in the ignition.

By the time he returned to the house and the communications room, Kurtzman had completed his data transfer. Bolan had a few words with the Stony Man computer expert before checking with Brognola.

"I'm leaving now," Bolan said. "I need to pick up the trail. Let the hour run out before you make your call."

Moments later the warrior was behind the wheel of the 4 × 4, following the narrow dirt road until it joined the highway some six miles on. He halted at the junction, deep in thought. On impulse he turned the vehicle to the north, in the direction that would take him to Montego Bay.

18

"I still don't understand what's going on," Robert Johnson complained.

"Don't ask. Just steer the goddamn boat," Hornaday snapped.

Johnson turned his attention to the moonlit swell of the Caribbean. Despite his misgivings, he did as he was told. He wasn't going to argue with Hornaday while the man was in his present mood. The merc's temper was teetering on the edge. He seemed about to explode with fury, just wanting something or someone to let fly at.

The American had been relaxing on board the *Cayman Queen* when Hornaday, Santos and the silent Korean, Shen, had shown up, along with Royal Doucette and his top man, Maurice. Hornaday, striding into the cabin, had demanded that Johnson take them out to sea, after inquiring whether the cruiser was fully fuelled.

"Sure," Johnson had replied. "I always keep her fully tanked. Why?"

Hornaday had given him a shove in the direction of the wheelhouse.

"Because we're going on a trip is why."

"Where to?"

"Nassau," Hornaday had snapped. "Now fire up this tub and let's get the hell under way. Shen, get the lines."

The Korean had obediently cast off the fore and aft lines.

Hornaday had dumped a long canvas bag on the cabin floor. He unzipped it and took out an Uzi. Johnson watched as the merc loaded the weapon and cocked it.

"Yeah, it's that time," Hornaday had said, catching Johnson's anxious stare. "Let's go, hotshot."

Now they were just under an hour out of Montego Bay, the cruiser gliding smoothly over the water.

Santos appeared in the wheelhouse. It was the first time Johnson had seen the Colombian since he had come on board. The man looked troubled.

"Can't you tell me what's happened?" Johnson asked.

Santos sat down, staring angrily across at Hornaday.

"You want to know? I will tell you, Robert. The man who attacked up at the docks raided the base. He cleared the place out. Killed anyone who got in his way—my people and Brett's celebrated professionals. We barely escaped."

Johnson made no comment. A flippant "I told you so" would have got him a bullet in the back of the head from Hornaday.

"Why are we going to Nassau?" he inquired cautiously.

Santos glanced across at Hornaday. "I'm interested in the reason for that myself. Are we just running, or do you have pressing business there?"

"The fact that you fucked up in Jamaica, Rio, means we have to clear out for now. The operation has gone completely. Once the news gets back to Medellín that you've lost the Caribbean connection, the cartel isn't going to be pleased. If I can take out LeGault, then I retain my credibility to some degree. It's all I've got left. I'm not going to the wall for you. Sorry, Rio, but we live in a hard world."

Santos restrained himself with a great effort. His eyes held little compassion for Hornaday.

"The fact that I personally put your name forward to lead the strike team means nothing?"

Hornaday smiled coldly. "Hell, yes. Sure, I'm grateful. It doesn't mean I have to go down with you. I've got to think of my future. Icing LeGault should buy me some brownie points with Medellín. Look at it this way—at least you haven't been a complete failure. I'm going to make you proud of me."

Santos lost control. He shoved up off the seat, his right hand sliding under his jacket for the pistol he carried.

Off to his left he spotted movement. The Colombian's head snapped around, terror flaring in his eyes when he saw the powerful figure of Shen reaching out for him. The Korean had entered the wheelhouse on silent feet, placing himself unobtrusively behind Santos.

The Colombian kept reaching for the gun, desperately trying to avoid Shen's huge, gnarled hands. The weapon was his only chance. He didn't get to touch the gun.

Shen's thick fingers closed over his wrist, crushing tightly. Santos threw an ineffectual punch at Shen's face, but the Korean simply leaned back from the clenched fist. His own left hand lashed out, knuckles cracking against Santos's face. The Colombian's nose vanished in a bright spurt of blood. With barely an effort Shen swung the man across the wheelhouse. Santos, unable to halt his headlong flight, smashed into the far wall. He stumbled and fell, groaning in agony.

Before he could recover, Shen had reached him. The Korean dragged his quarry to his feet, locking his right arm up his back. With deliberate and methodical precision Shen used the hardened edge of his right hand to hit Santos. The blows were delivered with brutal force. The Colombian cried out in pain as his ribs cracked, the blows causing internal injuries. Blood began to trickle from his slack lips. By this time Santos had lost consciousness. He slumped in Shen's grip, but the Korean's impressive strength kept him upright.

"Jesus," Johnson whispered. "The guy's had enough, Hornaday."

The merc simply waved the Uzi at him.

"Stick to being a sailor." He caught the Korean's attention. "Finish him, Shen."

The impassive Korean took Santos's limp form in his massive hands. Gripping the Colombian's head, he gave it a sudden twist. There was a muted crunching sound. Santos jerked, then sagged.

"You got any problems with this?" Hornaday asked Doucette.

The Jamaican shook his head. "I always thought he'd come to a bad end. Pity it ended this way, 'cause I was starting to make good. Now what have I got?"

"You got me, Royal, and I'm still running things. Hang in and I'll see you don't lose. Once I finish this job in Nassau, we'll talk. Meantime I need you to do some baby-sitting for me."

The merc was looking at Johnson as he spoke.

"Sure thing," Doucette said. "We'll handle that."

Hornaday turned to Shen, waving a hand in the corpse's direction. "Wrap something heavy around his feet and dump him over the side."

Shen left the wheelhouse with his grisly burden.

Hornaday moved to stand beside Johnson. He gazed out through the windshield.

"I have a feeling we understand each other a little better now, Bob," he said softly. "You agree?"

Johnson nodded. There was a cold, greasy feeling in the pit of his stomach. He couldn't bring himself to speak. He realized how close he was to death himself. The game, which had seemed exciting, almost glamorous, had suddenly turned sour. Johnson was in the real world, and it was cold, dark and not very friendly.

As far as he could see, there didn't seem to be a way out.

Not alive. So for the time being he would do exactly what Hornaday told him to do.

BOLAN'S INTUITION DREW him to the quayside where the *Cayman Queen* was usually berthed. Johnson's cruiser wasn't in the bay. Bolan stood at the water's edge, frustrated. He was convinced now that his guess had been right. Brett Hornaday and his surviving associates had taken Johnson's cruiser and were on their way to Nassau. The merc had lost his battle for Jamaica, but he would still want his moment of triumph.

And that would come with the assassination of Jack LeGault.

As the warrior walked back to where he had parked the 4×4, he noticed a lean, gray-haired Jamaican watching him. The man was leaning against a wall, a thin cigar dangling from his lips.

"You lookin' for something, mister?"

Bolan nodded. "The *Cayman Queen.*"

"You're too late. She left a couple hours ago. In a hurry, too. That Johnson fellow, he had visitors sudden like. They all jumped on board and next thing that boat, she was gone."

Bolan climbed into the 4×4 and started the engine. He drove away from the quayside, taking the vehicle into the darkness beyond the brightly lighted bay area. He spotted a pay phone at a gas station and pulled over. Moments later he had Brognola on the line and made a simple request. He needed a quick exit from Jamaica, an arranged, unofficial flight to Nassau and a contact on New Providence Island who could point him in the right direction.

"No questions on this one," Bolan added. "Trust me, Hal, I just need to get to Nassau. One of the agencies must have an undercover contact on Jamaica. Use your clout and get me a ride. And I need some extra firepower."

Hal Brognola sensed the urgency in Bolan's voice. He had his own ideas as to why the Executioner wanted to reach Nassau without showing his hand. The big Fed didn't question those reasons. He had reached an understanding with Bolan a long time ago, leaving the final decisions on missions to the man's own judgment.

"Leave it with me, Striker. I'll have you an answer within the hour."

BROGNOLA'S CONTACT MAN proved to be exactly what Mack Bolan needed, providing what the Executioner wanted without question. By late morning the following day Bolan was in the passenger seat of a twin-engined airplane, being flown to the Bahamas.

The contact, who was also the pilot, had turned out to be a lanky, blond-haired American in his mid-thirties. He reminded Bolan of a young James Stewart. Lean and monosyllabic, yet possessing a depth of intelligence and perception beyond his years. His name was Hardin. When he spoke his accent suggested the Southwestern area of the U.S.A., and it was easy to imagine him crossing the dusty range on a slow pony.

"Not the first time you've handled this kind of thing," Bolan said.

Hardin gave one of his infrequent smiles. "Keeps the days interesting," he remarked. "By the way I was told to give you this."

He handed Bolan a zippered carryall. Inside was a 9 mm Uzi and a stack of spare magazines.

"Thanks," the warrior said, closing the bag.

All he got was a noncommittal shrug.

Bolan took the opportunity to get some rest. It was only now, with the high of the past couple of days fading away, that he realized just how tired he was. He had been using and abusing his body constantly, with little letup. The effect was beginning to take hold. Sleep came easily. Bolan let it steal over him, grateful for the calm in the middle of the storm.

He opened his eyes as the pitch of the plane's engines changed. He could feel the aircraft beginning to descend. Glancing out the side port, he saw the brilliant sea glittering in the morning sunlight. Just ahead was the coastline of New Providence, the island where Nassau was situated. Hardin was taking the plane down to a soft landing on a strip of white beach fringed by slanting palms. After touchdown the pilot cruised to a halt, turning the craft for its takeoff.

"That's your guy," he said, pointing to where a man had stepped out from the shadow of the palms.

Bolan climbed down from the aircraft, his bag in his hand.

"So long." The pilot raised a brown hand.

Bolan nodded and closed the cabin door, stepping away from the plane as Hardin revved the engines. The plane rolled out along the beach, lifting swiftly into the empty sky.

"Mr. Belasko?"

The Executioner turned to face the speaker. The man wore a light suit and a shirt with a tie. Bolan knew the guy had to be British.

"I'm Will Harrow. Shall we go?"

There was a gleaming car waiting on the far side of the trees. In moments they were in the vehicle and heading toward Nassau.

"Anything I need to know?" Bolan asked.

"The *Cayman Queen* is at its usual berth in the harbor. She arrived around eleven this morning. I can't tell you how many are on board. If Johnson brought people in, they either slipped ashore before he reached harbor, or left the boat before I located her."

"That was what I was afraid of," Bolan said. "What about Jack LeGault?"

"Staying at the Atlantis on West Bay Street. He has two of his agents with him. From what Washington told me he'll be here for two days, discussing upcoming operations against the drug traffickers with the Bahamian drug squad."

"Where are the talks taking place?"

"That seems to be a well-kept secret," Harrow replied. "Even I can't find that out. I'll keep trying."

"Okay," Bolan said. "Anything else?"

"I've got a small apartment for you," the Briton replied. "I realize you might not be using it very much, but at least it will give you a chance to freshen up."

Harrow pulled a set of keys from his pocket. "One for the apartment. There's a basement garage. You'll find a car there if you need it. Nothing special in looks, but the engine has been fine-tuned, so keep a light foot on the gas pedal."

"I'll try to remember."

"There's a bag behind your seat. Got some things in it that might be of help," Harrow suddenly said after they had been driving for a while.

The bag held fresh clothing and shoes. There was even a wallet containing cash. Bolan also noticed a card with a telephone number written on it.

"You can contact me on that number day or night."

"Could be useful," Bolan murmured as he pocketed the card. "Thanks."

"Thank your friend in Washington who set all this up. He was most insistent I arrange those things for you. You obviously know some very influential people, Mr. Belasko."

They reached Nassau within the hour. Harrow drove along Bay Street, with the sparkling waters of Nassau Bay on their left. In the middle of the bay lay Paradise Island, joined to the mainland by the Paradise Bridge. The island was a haven of luxury hotels and even had its own golf course.

The bay was crowded with boats of all shapes and sizes, including the *Cayman Queen*. Harrow pointed out Robert Johnson's cruiser as he drove past the berths. A few minutes later the Briton drew to a halt outside a white-painted apartment building on a shady street off the harbor front.

Bolan climbed out, taking his bags with him.

"I'll keep in touch," Harrow said. "If I pick up anything useful I'll pass it along. Apart from that I stay out of your way."

The Executioner nodded. "Probably a wise move," he said, shaking the Briton's hand.

He watched Harrow drive away, then turned and walked up the steps and into the building, taking the stairs to the floor where his apartment was located. Inside he dumped the bags and checked out the modest but comfortable accommodation.

He found the bathroom, stripped off his clothing, turned on the shower and stepped under it. He soaped himself clean, then allowed the warm water to cascade over his tired body for a long time. Stepping out, he searched the bathroom medicine chest for a razor and a can of foam. When he'd finished shaving he slipped into the cotton robe hanging behind the door and wandered through to the small kitchen. The fridge was well stocked, and Bolan poured himself a tall glass of orange juice.

The apartment's front windows gave him an unrestricted view of the harbor front, and he stood watching the peaceful scene.

He wondered idly where Hornaday was. The merc had come to Nassau in order to carry out his contract on Jack LeGault. The how and the where needed to be answered. Perhaps Robert Johnson could give the Executioner those answers.

Bolan drained the glass of orange juice. He felt the need to be on the move.

He opened the bag Harrow had given him and pulled out the clothes it contained. Laying them out, he noticed that the sizes were all correct. He had Hal Brognola to thank for that. The warrior dressed and quickly pulled on the shoulder rig holding the Beretta. He shrugged on a light jacket over the weapon, jammed the wallet into his back pocket and let himself out of the apartment.

Once on the street he walked in the direction of the harbor, his destination the *Cayman Queen*.

Bolan needed to get on board the cruiser.

And hopefully have a talk with Robert Johnson.

19

The *Cayman Queen* was tied up at the far end of the quay. There were three empty berths between the cruiser and the other vessels. The sleek craft rode the gentle swell in isolation. Bolan made his way along the jetty, approaching the cruiser with caution. His eyes scanned the vessel's deck and superstructure. He saw no sign of movement and began to wonder if there was anyone on board at all.

He stepped up the companionway attached to the cruiser's side and went on board. Silence greeted him. The warrior slipped the Beretta from its holster as he neared the main hatch, keeping the weapon at his side. He slipped through the opening and moved along the passage that led toward the main cabin. It looked exactly as it had when he had viewed it from the overhead skylight. The only difference was the fact that this time it was deserted. The chairs around the long table were empty.

Bolan retraced his steps, easing along the deck. He decided to check out the wheelhouse. Pushing open the door, he saw Robert Johnson seated by the cruiser's control panel. The Executioner slipped inside the wheelhouse, closing the door behind him. The soft click alerted Johnson. He swiveled the leather chair and stared across the wheelhouse at Bolan. The expression in the man's eyes warned Bolan things weren't as they seemed.

"You shouldn't have come," Johnson warned, his voice trembling. His eyes stared beyond Bolan. The Executioner realized his error a fraction of a second too late.

The hard metal ring of a gun muzzle jabbed against his spine, grinding into his flesh.

Bolan had been drawn into a neat setup.

The insistent gun muzzle jabbed again. Reluctantly the warrior allowed the Beretta to slip from his fingers to the deck of the wheelhouse. A hand flattened against his back and pushed him forward to stand beside Johnson. Bolan turned slowly and looked at his captor.

He stared into the impassive brown face of the Jamaican hood, Royal Doucette. Just behind Doucette was the guy Bolan had faced down outside Winston Rogers's apartment. Both men held guns.

"You," Doucette ordered, glancing at Johnson. "Start the engine."

Johnson did as he was told.

Maurice picked up Bolan's Beretta and tucked it under his belt.

"Maurice, get outside and cast off."

When Maurice returned to the wheelhouse Doucette caught Johnson's attention.

"Get us away from the bay. Take her out to deep water."

Johnson eased open the throttle and took the cruiser out of the berth. Under Doucette's direction he sailed the *Cayman Queen* out of the harbor. The gang leader waited until they were well clear of the island and any other craft before he ordered Johnson to drop anchor and cut the engine. As the soft pulse of sound faded, Bolan turned his attention to his captor.

"Now what?" Bolan asked.

Maurice, who had regained his courage since his previous encounter with the warrior, crossed to stand in front of the tall American.

"Now, Yank, you don't look so damn tough to me. Man, you don't look like nothin'. And you'll look even less when we drop you dead in the water."

"Where's Hornaday?" Bolan asked, ignoring Maurice's grinning face.

Johnson glanced at Doucette, who remained silent.

"Somewhere ashore. That's all I know," Johnson said.

"He still intend to kill Jack LeGault?"

"You know the answer to that. It's why you followed him."

"I had you pegged as being too smart to get caught up with murder," Bolan commented.

"I had no choice," Johnson said bitterly. "Santos wasn't taken with the idea, so Hornaday had him killed."

"Hornaday wants to keep in with the cartel, so he goes through with his contract. Is that the idea?"

Johnson nodded.

"He must know by now that I've alerted LeGault. But he's still going ahead. I wouldn't have put him down as suicidal."

"Not suicidal," Johnson said. "But mad as hell because of what you did to his people."

The Executioner concealed his reaction to the comment. Surely that wasn't the reason why Hornaday was still going for LeGault, because he knew Bolan would try to stop him. And that would give Hornaday the opportunity to kill Bolan.

Was it as simple as that, Hornaday wanted revenge, his desire to pay back Bolan for destroying his strike team and making the merc look incompetent?

Bolan knew that losing face and being made to look stupid could leave people with a rage that could only be extinguished by hitting back at the person responsible.

He wouldn't have expected such a reaction from a man who considered himself a professional. Oddly, though, individual perceptions concerning the word "professional" differed widely. So the behavior of people could vary.

Hornaday, it appeared, had decided to carry out his contract killing of Jack LeGault, and possibly engineer the death of the man he blamed for the downfall of his strike force.

If the facts were true, then Bolan had problems. Because he wasn't going to be able to stop Hornaday while he remained on Johnson's cruiser under the watchful eye of Royal Doucette and his henchman.

Bolan glanced at Doucette. The Jamaican hadn't moved from his earlier position. The gun in his hands remained on-target, and the warrior wondered how proficient the man was with the weapon.

The range was close.

The possibility was slim, but Bolan decided it was worth exploiting.

But how?

Robert Johnson provided the catalyst for the action that followed.

"Royal, I've had enough of this sitting around," he stated suddenly, his voice breaking the silence.

The Jamaican turned his head slightly.

"You stay where you are."

"The hell I will. This is my damn boat, and I don't give a shit for your games."

Johnson stood up as he spoke. His face was flushed with frustration. He was scared but also angry.

His sudden move caused Doucette to shift the muzzle of the gun he was holding. The weapon swung around to cover Johnson.

Bolan saw the weapon move away from him. It was his opportunity, probably the only chance he'd get. Risky or not, he had to make it work.

Maurice was closest to Bolan, and even he had averted his gaze, interest over Johnson making him lax.

Pushing away from the bulkhead, the Executioner snatched at a fire extinguisher held in a clip mounted on the wall. He gripped it by the nozzle and swung it clublike. The metal cylinder caught Maurice across the back of the skull before he had time to face Bolan's attack. He swung the extinguisher again, a glancing blow to Maurice's forehead that pushed the Jamaican against the bulkhead.

The gang leader was knocked off balance by Bolan's move, his handgun wavering as he tried to regain control. Bolan didn't allow him the opportunity. He lashed out with his left foot, catching Doucette in the groin. The Jamaican doubled over, the gun in his fist sagging to the deck. As the hardman lowered his head, the Executioner jerked up his knee to meet it. The connection was hard, Doucette's face flowering with bright blood from his crushed nose and mouth. The force of the blow hurled him across the wheelhouse.

Maurice had recovered, and raised his gun. Bolan lashed out with his fist, knocking the weapon away. The Jamaican muttered angrily, but made no attempt to retrieve the weapon. His right hand slid under his jacket, reappearing with a switchblade. The slim knife flashed into view. Maurice lunged at Bolan, cutting the air in vicious arcs. The Executioner stepped back, allowing Maurice to complete a cut, then stepped in fast before the Jamaican could reverse the move. He grabbed the Jamaican's knife wrist, pulling it in tight against his side. With his free hand he drove a hard fist into Maurice's body, then swung the man in a half circle, slamming him against Doucette.

Bolan, still on the move, closed in again on Maurice as the man regained his balance. The Jamaican still held the knife. He shook his head wildly, trying to rid himself of the blood that was streaming into his eyes from the deep cut in his forehead.

"Son of a bitch," he screamed, his voice shrill with rage. He hurled himself at Bolan, the knife out in front like a small saber. He was wide open, and the Executioner used the man's anger, sidestepping his rush easily. He kicked up into Maurice's exposed stomach, bringing the man to his knees. He snaked an arm around the Jamaican's neck, grabbing his collar and pulling hard across his throat.

Maurice began to choke, and he waved the knife, trying to cut his foe. Bolan's free hand caught the wrist. He applied pressure, his fingers digging in to maintain a sound grip while he increased his stranglehold. Maurice continued to struggle, which only added to his discomfort. Bolan forced his knife wrist down, turning the blade in toward the man's body until he was able to push the knife in under Maurice's ribs and into the heart. The Jamaican stiffened, his whole body arching in agony. Then he fell facedown on the deck as Bolan let go of him.

As Maurice dropped, the Executioner slid his fingers around the butt of the Beretta and pulled it from the Jamaican's belt. He turned to Doucette and was in time to see the Jamaican vanishing through the wheelhouse door.

The Jamaican got off a rapid trio of shots just before he slipped from sight.

Bolan heard an odd sound and glanced over his shoulder. Robert Johnson was down. He had his hands clasped over his face and throat, and blood slipped between his splayed fingers where Doucette's bullets had struck home.

The wheelhouse windows erupted, showering glass across the interior as the Jamaican laid down another close-spaced volley of shots.

Bolan dropped to the deck, crawling for the door. He kept low, using the door for cover as he rolled onto the deck.

From the position of the shots, he knew that Doucette had been heading for the cruiser's stern. The reason hit Bolan instantly. The Jamaican was trying for the small dinghy secured at the rear of the aft deck. If he could get that into the water he might escape.

The warrior moved along the deck, the Beretta tracking ahead of him. He reached the aft section of the superstructure and peered around the bulkhead.

Doucette was waiting, crouched beside the dinghy. He fired several shots, the slugs digging long slivers of wood from the bulkhead timber. Bolan pulled his head down. He extended his hand and triggered a 3-round burst at the dinghy, which chewed into its fiberglass hull. Bolan heard a frantic scrambling as Doucette became aware of his vulnerable position. The Jamaican hood realized that the dinghy's thin hull wasn't going to provide much in the way of protective cover.

Bolan kept up his barrage of shots, spacing the bursts the length of the dinghy, driving Doucette to one end. The Jamaican, sensing the inevitable confrontation, fed a fresh clip into the butt of his handgun, cocked the weapon and came out shooting. He drove shot after shot at Bolan's position as he made a dash for better cover.

The Executioner caught him in midstride. The Jamaican's body jerked awkwardly as a burst of 9 mm subsonic rounds cored into his flesh, burning deep. He fell headlong, blood spidering across the deck.

Bolan checked to confirm the man was dead before he returned to the wheelhouse. Robert Johnson lay unconscious on the deck. He had taken a bullet in the face and another in the throat. The man was having trouble breathing.

Under Bolan's guidance the cruiser began to move, slowly, gaining speed as he swung her about. He brought the *Cayman Queen* under control and took her in a slow curve toward her berth.

Once he had the cruiser tied up, Bolan went to the nearest pay phone, dialed the emergency service and called for an ambulance, giving the operator the information that would lead the medical crew to the *Cayman Queen*. That accomplished, the warrior slipped away from the quayside and returned to the apartment. As he climbed the stairs he heard the wail of an ambulance.

After letting himself in, Bolan picked up the telephone and made a call to Stony Man Farm. He settled in a comfortable chair as the number was redirected and fed through the electronic security system. Though the SOG tried to maintain tight control over the communications system, everyone realized that totally secure lines were sometimes difficult to achieve.

Barbara Price came on the line. Despite the urgency of the moment, Bolan experienced a feeling of regret at not being in the presence of the lovely young woman. Since joining the Stony Man team, Price had become close to Mack Bolan—as close as he would allow anyone during his seemingly eternal battle. He had cast aside the warrior's role for a few brief moments of pleasure in her company during his infrequent visits to the Farm. Despite the feelings they had experienced, neither of them had committed themselves to anything permanent, being content in the joy of the moment and the possibility of future meetings. Price was as dedicated in her role of mission controller as Bolan in his, so she was aware of the need for no strings when it came to relationships.

"Hi," she said, recognizing his voice the moment he spoke. "How are things?"

"Okay," he replied. "I need to speak to the man."

"Trouble?"

"I could do with some official string-pulling."

Moments later Brognola's heavy voice rumbled down the line. "What gives, Striker?"

Bolan quickly detailed the events since his arrival in Nassau.

"I'm going to want some official clout backing me," Bolan concluded. "The local cops are going to want some answers about a couple of dead Jamaicans and a badly injured American, but I don't have the time to explain. This has to be hard and fast. I've got to bypass the red tape. Can you clear a way for me? Make it so I get police assistance and not stonewalling?"

"Sit tight. I'll have Harrow with you as soon as I can clear this. How bad is it?"

"All I can tell you for sure is we have a cartel enforcer loose on the island. He's gunning for Jack LeGault, and he wants to flush me out at the same time."

"Hang in there, Striker."

Bolan put down the telephone. He crossed to the kitchen and put water on to boil. He found a jar of instant coffee in a cupboard, and when the water boiled he made himself a mug of strong, black coffee.

He pulled the Uzi from his bag, loaded the weapon and slipped a spare magazine into the inside pocket of his jacket. He added a couple of spares for the 93-R, as well.

His impatience was growing. Bolan was aware of the difficulties of arranging official cooperation, but his inner clock was counting off the falling numbers, numbers that were reminding him of the threat to Jack LeGault.

Bolan snatched up the telephone the second it rang.

It was Brognola, and his tone was grim.

"Striker, we just got word. LeGault's missing from his hotel. His two bodyguards have been found dead, both taken out with bullets in the back of their heads. No sign of Jack. No one saw or heard anything."

Bolan's hand squeezed tight against the receiver.

Hornaday had already made his move.

He had Jack LeGault, and he was using him as bait to draw the Executioner out into the open. Otherwise he would have completed his kill the moment he had laid eyes on the man.

There was no more time for debate. Mack Bolan had to accept Hornaday's challenge if he was to pull Jack LeGault out alive.

The lines were in motion, coming together.

Reaching kill point.

20

Paul Sanderson, the Bahamian police sergeant who accompanied Bolan to the hospital, made no effort to conceal his distaste for the task. It was obvious that he had been given his orders by a higher authority, and those orders had said for him to cooperate with the American.

"This way," he snapped as he led Bolan through the hospital. "The doctor in charge isn't going to be very happy about this."

"I'm not here to make his day. All I need are a few minutes with Johnson. Then I'm out of here."

The sergeant's wide shoulders hunched, but he refrained from further comment.

Bolan followed him along the corridor. A uniformed cop stood outside the door to Johnson's room.

Sanderson flashed his ID. "We need to go in."

"Doctor's in there now," the cop replied.

Bolan pushed open the door and went in.

"What's going on here?" the white-coated doctor demanded. He lowered the clipboard he was writing on. "Just who are you people?"

Sanderson flashed his ID again. "Official police business, Doctor. And before you say anything to me, I suggest you check with the hospital administrator. He's had *his* orders, too."

"Are you joking?" the doctor asked. "This man only came out of surgery a couple of hours ago. I took a bullet out of his face and another from his throat. He might not live. Do you understand that? Good God, man, he can barely talk."

"Just a couple of minutes, Doctor," Bolan said. "Then we'll leave."

"I won't let this rest here. You have no right. No right at all."

The medic retreated, angry, but familiar with "official" orders. He closed the door behind him.

Bolan crossed to the bed where Robert Johnson lay.

The man looked terrible. The left side of his face was swathed in bandages, which extended down and across his throat. Tubes fed to his body, connected to drips. Johnson's vital signs were displayed on the glowing screens of monitors surrounding his bed.

Johnson's exposed right eye was open, and he watched Bolan closely. He was only just coming out of the anesthetic.

"Are those Jamaican bastards dead?" Johnson asked. His voice came from the grave, a slurred, croaking whisper that obviously hurt like hell.

Bolan simply nodded.

"I owe you for that."

"I'm here to collect," Bolan told him.

Johnson acknowledged with a flick of his finger.

"Hornaday has snatched Jack LeGault and disappeared. Where would he take him? Does he have a base here on New Providence?"

Johnson indicated he wanted a pad and pencil. The sergeant handed over his own. The man wrote laboriously, stopping as weariness threatened. Finally he handed the pad to Bolan. The Executioner read the scrawled message. "Only place I can think of. Villa at Lyford Cay. Cartel bought it. Safehouse. I arranged deal."

"You know it?" Bolan asked the police sergeant.

Sanderson nodded. "A place for the very rich. Out of my league."

Johnson took the pad back and wrote the address. He seemed to sink into the bed, looking very tired.

"Let's go," Bolan said.

"I don't suppose you want any kind of official backup on this?" Sanderson asked.

"No way."

The Executioner walked out of the room and left the hospital, followed by the sergeant. Outside they crossed to the unmarked police car that had been provided along with Sanderson. Bolan slid into the passenger seat. As Sanderson settled behind the wheel, he glanced at Bolan.

"This man, Hornaday. Is he dangerous?"

"Yeah. He'll kill without giving it a second's thought. Anyone who gets in his way."

Sanderson grumbled angrily as he started the car and rolled it out of the parking lot.

"I don't like these bastards bringing their mess to my island. Let them stay in their own damn countries."

"I wish it was that way. But places like Nassau will always attract these people. It's the money they come for. The crowds of people looking for a new experience. And drugs still have a fashionable attraction for some people. As long as the demand is there, you'll have the traffickers."

"Not if I was running things," Sanderson said, wheeling the car around a minivan. "I don't care who hears me say it. If I had my way I'd stand them all against a wall and shoot the bunch of them. No damn question about it—I'd shoot them all."

"You'll get no argument from me there. You people have to handle the mess these traffickers leave behind. The dead and the wounded. No one should have to deal with that. But it'll go on until the drug war's won. If it ever is."

The exchange broke the icy reserve the cop had erected between himself and Bolan. Although he didn't probe too deeply about the Executioner's business, Sanderson mellowed a little. Bolan understood the cop's earlier antagonism. New Providence was Sanderson's beat. It was his turf, and to have some stranger walk in and take charge, making Sanderson play second fiddle, had to hurt.

Bolan had driven home the point during his meeting with Sanderson's superiors. The only chance LeGault had of surviving was for Bolan to face Hornaday on a one-to-one basis. The Executioner read the merc's position. The man *had* to be seen to be handling the situation by himself. Against all the odds. His reputation depended on that confrontation with Bolan. If Hornaday won, then his future was comparatively secure. If he lost, it wouldn't matter because he would be dead. The merc knew and accepted that. He was willing to put his life on the line. Jack LeGault was the pawn in the middle of the game. Hornaday wouldn't give a damn about the DEA agent's life. Bolan, on the other hand, cared a great deal. LeGault's existence depended on him, and he couldn't have ignored that even if he wanted to.

Lyford Cay's sprawl of villas, basking beneath the warmth of the Bahamian sun, exuded an atmosphere of wealth and luxury. Sanderson cruised along the approach to the complex, parking in the first space he found.

Bolan followed the sergeant as he led the way to the villa. They studied the place from a distance.

"No easy way to handle this," Sanderson said. "If he's waiting for you, there's no telling what he might have planned."

The warrior had been checking the area out. He agreed with Sanderson's observation. On the other hand he saw no point in waiting. Hornaday wasn't going to push the situation. He was going to sit and wait for Bolan to make *his* move.

"I'm going in," the Executioner announced. "The longer we wait, the more likely he might do something to LeGault. I don't want that to happen on my account."

"Let me back you up," Sanderson said.

Bolan shook his head.

"Not a good idea. Hornaday and his Korean shadow are professionals at killing. It's the way they make their living. Doesn't matter who or how. Blink an eye and they'll nail you."

Leaving the policeman on the street, the warrior circled the villa, using every inch of cover he could, and approached the building from the back. There was a paved rear area, filled with luxuriant plants and flowers. The warm air was heavy with the overpowering scent of the exotic blooms.

Once he was within the confines of the garden, Bolan unclipped the Uzi from its shoulder strap beneath his jacket and began to close in on the house. He took his time, checking before he moved ahead, assessing each section first, his eyes taking in the details of the area.

Nothing moved, but there was a silence about the place that Bolan found far from natural.

There was the possibility that Hornaday wasn't in the house at all. Johnson's information might have been incorrect. For all Bolan knew the merc could be somewhere else on the island.

He still had to check the place out, if only to eliminate it.

There was a patio just ahead. On the other side lay the rear wall of the villa. A tinted picture window with sliding glass doors took up the greater part of the back wall.

Bolan moved to the side, approaching the doors at an angle.

Something caught his eye, and the warrior dropped into a crouch. A thin, almost-invisible strip of monofilament was stretched tautly across the path at his feet. He leaned across, peering into the green swell of vegetation into which the strand vanished, and saw the fragmentation grenade wired to a wooden stake wedged in the earth. Pressure on the filament would have pulled the grenade's pin, already worked to the limit. The grenade would have been set on a two- or three-second fuse. Scant time when it came to escaping the bomb's blast.

Finding the booby trap confirmed Hornaday's presence. The merc had devised a security shield around the villa.

Bolan immediately thought about Sanderson. He turned, glancing back the way he'd come. Sure enough, the sergeant's bulky form crouched at the base of a sculpted ornamental pot that held a profusion of brilliant blooms.

Retracing his steps, the Executioner began to work his way toward Sanderson. The cop watched him, a puzzled expression on his face. He wasn't sure why

Bolan was returning, and for some reason decided to move out to meet him.

Sanderson had only moved a couple of feet when the near silence of the peaceful garden was broken by the low stutter of suppressed autofire.

Bolan dropped flat to the ground. He heard the thump of bullets striking stonework and the sound of others striking human flesh.

Sanderson gave a hoarse grunt. His handgun clattered to the ground, followed by the impact of a body.

The Executioner raised his head and saw the sergeant sprawled on the ground. The cop's left hand was stretched out, his fingers clawing at the stone path. Bolan could see the pattern of bright blood marking Sanderson's jacket.

He reached the Bahamian policeman, caught hold of his lapel and dragged the wounded man into the cover of a raised stone plant trough. Rolling Sanderson onto his back, Bolan saw the bloody patch staining his shirtfront. He had caught a number of bullets in his left upper chest and shoulder. From the way Sanderson's arm lay, it looked as if the bone were broken.

"Jesus, man it bloody well hurts!" Sanderson whispered. His face gleamed with sweat, his eyes revealing the pain that racked his body. "He really caught me, huh?"

"This should get you some R and R on the beach."

"That really consoles me. Look, Belasko, get the hell after him. I'll be fine."

"You're bleeding all over the place."

"I got plenty. Dammit, man, go after your merc before we get anyone else hurt. I can look after myself."

Bolan turned and made his way along the path toward the house. He changed course after a few yards, slipping into the thick, tall cluster of flowers and ferns that comprised the wide, curving floral display close to the perimeter fence. The interwoven canopy of greenery closed over his head, and the warrior breathed in the earthy aroma of soil and vegetation. It was almost like being deep in the jungle. He brought his combat skills into play, moving along the thick bed of plants with the ease of a shadow. He was able to reach the corner of the house without drawing any fire.

The patio lay a couple of yards away, the glass doors reflecting the brilliant sunshine. Bolan eased out of the greenery, stepping onto the patterned stones of the patio, then flattened himself against the stone pillars flanking the picture window.

The shots that had downed Sanderson hadn't come through the sliding doors. Bolan had been facing them when the shooting started, and he knew the doors hadn't opened. That meant Hornaday or Shen was positioned at another window. The only one Bolan had seen on this end of the house was a small one over on the far side. It had frosted glass in the main panel, which suggested a bathroom.

The warrior bent and picked up a couple of large pebbles from the edging around the flower bed. He tossed one into the thick ferns near the center of the garden area, causing the greenery to move and rustle.

The subdued burst of gunfire that followed, sending a stream of bullets into the foliage, *did* come from the window he had pinpointed. Bolan's keen eyes spotted the heavy tube of a suppressor poking through the opened upper panel.

Without warning, Sanderson opened fire, a steady volley of shots that peppered the stonework around the frosted window. The final bullet took out the glass itself. Bolan saw the suppressor draw back.

The Executioner sprinted across the patio and tried the sliding doors. They were locked. He didn't hesitate, raising the Uzi and triggering a short burst that shattered the glass. Bolan went through the opening and into the wide, airy lounge beyond. He crossed the room in long strides, flattening against the wall to one side of the half-open door.

He waited for a few seconds, then ducked and went through, the Uzi tracking ahead of him. A staircase to his right led to the upper floor. An archway allowed access to the house on the other side of the stairs, cutting beneath the staircase itself.

As the warrior moved toward the archway, he saw a brief flicker of shadow. Then the suppressed subgun opened up. A sustained burst of 9 mm rounds hammered the wall above Bolan's head, showering him with slivers of plaster. He stepped to the side of the archway and the gunner let loose again. More slugs peppered the wall, shredding an oil painting that hung there.

Bolan triggered a burst from the Uzi, the slugs digging into the wall just inside the arch, ripping holes and exposing the mortar beneath the white plaster. The moment he'd fired, Bolan went for the archway.

The clatter of running feet told him somebody was on the move, which suited Bolan. A running man had little opportunity to offer resistance.

The short passage beneath the staircase opened into a small empty room. At the far end a part-open door revealed the pristine dimensions of a washroom. There was a passage off to the left.

Bolan heard the click of a weapon being cocked as he rounded the corner. He dropped to one knee a fraction of a second before the spray of shots chewed at the wall, his forward movement slamming him against the opposite wall. He twisted his body, thrusting the Uzi before him. He caught a glimpse of a darting figure pushing through a door at the end of the passage. Bolan rolled to his feet, sprinting to the door. He eased around the frame, peering into the large room.

It was devoid of furniture, but stacked with a number of packing cases.

Bolan had barely stepped up to the open door when a shape loomed on his right, coming from the wall just inside and to the right of the door. Powerful hands grabbed the warrior's jacket and hauled him over the threshold. Before he could react, Bolan was hurled bodily across the room. He crashed into the closest of the packing cases, the impact stunning him, the Uzi slipping from his fingers. Then he was preoccupied with protecting himself from the uppermost cases of the stack as they tumbled over him. Sharp edges bruised his flesh. Another caught the side of his face, opening a ragged gash.

Pushing aside the wooden cases, Bolan climbed to his feet and reached under his jacket for the Beretta, only to have it smashed from his hand by a massive gnarled fist.

Bolan raised his head, locking his gaze with that of the Korean, Shen.

Hornaday's bodyguard had tossed aside his own empty weapon and was resorting to the use of his own deadly weapons—his hands, toughened and conditioned by years of devoted practice.

The Executioner backpedaled, seeking a way to avoid Shen's clutches. He knew the man would be a formidable opponent.

Bolan's foot touched the edge of a packing case. He glanced down and saw that the top had become loose. He ducked, grabbed the top and swung it from floor-level, slashing for Shen's throat. The Korean simply swayed back out of harm's way. His muscular arms swept up, his hands attacking the wooden lid. His concentrated, precise blows shattered the lid as if it had been constructed from balsa wood.

The warrior was left with a single, jagged-edged slat in his right hand. He jabbed at Shen with it, and the Korean feinted, blocking the wooden stake with his upper arm. His free hand snaked forward, edge on. Bolan felt it strike the underside of his wrist. The blow numbed his hand and he dropped the stake.

Shen moved in fast now, seemingly intent on the kill. There was a deliberate change in his mood. The expression on his face seemed almost trancelike. It was his moment of full expression, when all of his training came into being.

Bolan turned to avoid Shen's first blow. He succeeded in avoiding the full impact. Even so, Shen's palm edge connected with the Executioner's side, delivering a hefty blow to his ribs. The pain was sudden and intense, causing Bolan to catch his breath.

Turning on his heel, the warrior retaliated with a sharp back kick. The toe of his shoe caught Shen under the right eye, gouging the flesh. Blood began to stream down the Korean's broad, angry face.

The moment he had delivered his kick, Bolan pulled back. He was playing for time. Even as he faced Shen, the Executioner was scanning the floor for either of his lost weapons. He located them both, deciding that the 93-R was closer. He made the Beretta his prime target.

Shen had other ideas. He launched himself at his adversary, moving with a speed seldom seen in a man of his bulk. With a sibilant hiss the Korean swept out his right arm, the back of his fist catching Bolan across the cheek.

The Executioner was knocked off balance, crashing against the wall and bouncing away. The follow-up was a stunning drive over Bolan's ribs that drove the air from his lungs. Shen turned in toward his victim, catching his body and spinning him over and across the room.

The warrior hit the floor, rolling out of control. He clawed at the floor, trying to halt his forward movement. His fingers brushed something hard and cold. He grasped it, pulling it close to his aching body as he realized that it was the Beretta.

He slid against the far wall, bumping to a sudden stop. He lay hunched over, his body crying out for relief, yet knowing that if he failed to react within the next few seconds he was going to be a dead man.

Out of the corner of his eye he sensed Shen's huge bulk approaching. Bolan slid the 93-R from its place of concealment, thrusting the muzzle up and out. His finger curled around the trigger.

There was so little time between the appearance of the weapon and its firing that Shen had no opportunity to turn aside. He just seemed to continue forward, directly into the path of the 3-round bursts that Bolan pumped into him. The Executioner kept on squeezing the trigger, the 9 mm slugs hammering into Shen's massive form, driving deep into the flesh. The Korean expelled a deep moan of pain as he fell forward, his huge hands outstretched and reaching for

Bolan even in his dying moments. He hit the floor with enough force to shake the building, twisting violently over onto his back, dead.

Mack Bolan climbed to his feet with great reluctance. His entire being pulsed with unrelenting pain. It hurt to move. It hurt more to walk. But walk he did, because he knew that the battle was far from over.

Somewhere in this house Brett Hornaday lay in wait for him. And the Executioner had no intention of leaving before he settled accounts with the man.

21

The ground floor of the villa was empty. Bolan made a sweep that took in the remaining rooms. He returned to the entrance lobby, and climbed the staircase swiftly, reaching the landing.

A wide hallway lay before him, doors opening onto various rooms. All the doors were closed—except one at the far end.

The warrior made his way along the passage, the Beretta held ready in his hand. He had decided to leave the Uzi behind, wanting to rely on the accuracy of the 93-R in a close combat situation. It was more than likely if he came face-to-face with Hornaday, that Jack LeGault would be nearby, perhaps being used as a shield by the merc. If that was the case, Bolan would need the controllable fire of the Beretta. With that in mind he flicked the selector on single-shot.

The open door beckoned silently, the room beyond spilling bright sunlight across the threshold.

The closer he got to the room, the more Bolan sensed the presence of someone inside.

He was no more than a couple of feet from the door when a voice reached out to him.

"No more time-wasting, Bolan. I'm here and so is LeGault, so don't try any stupid tricks."

Bolan registered the use of his name. He wondered how and where Hornaday had learned that. His curiosity was minimal.

He edged to the door, peering cautiously around the frame.

The room was wide and spacious, probably intended as the master bedroom. Now it was empty, the light spreading across the uncarpeted floor from the window that overlooked the rear area.

Two men stood close to the window.

The one Bolan judged to be Jack LeGault, tall and lean, was positioned directly in front of the second man. This one, tanned, with wolfish good looks, held a .357 Magnum revolver against the side of LeGault's head. Bolan noted that the DEA man's hands were cuffed together.

There was no way the warrior could make a killing shot. He lowered the Beretta, allowing the muzzle to point at the floor.

"I wanted you to see he was still alive," Hornaday said. "For the moment."

"So you can kill him now?" Bolan asked.

Hornaday actually smiled. "No one said it had to end happily."

He was watching Bolan closely, as if he were trying to read the Executioner's thoughts.

"I knew it had to be you," the former CIA agent said by way of explanation. "No one else could have come through all that shit the way you did. I told Spendloe it had to be Mack Bolan, and he finally admitted I was right. Too bad you killed him at the base. He would have appreciated seeing me take you out.''

"Is that what this is all about?" Bolan asked. "Your saving face so you can go back to the cartel?"

"What do you expect me to do, walk away and quit? No, mister, that isn't my way. I pay what's owed, and I finish my contracts. Only this time I take back a bonus. The head of Mack Bolan."

LeGault moved slightly. In response Hornaday jabbed the muzzle of the Magnum against his flesh, his left arm snaking around the DEA man's neck.

"Quit that, LeGault. We don't want to give Bolan any kind of edge, do we? I'll decide when it ends. Right, Bolan?"

"Belasko—Bolan—whatever your name is. Shoot the son of a bitch," LeGault said. "I'll take my chances. Just nail the bastard."

"Cut the crap, LeGault. Bolan isn't going to risk your life. The guy has a conscience. He won't let any good guys get killed on his account. Am I right?"

The Executioner didn't respond outwardly, but he knew Hornaday had him tagged. There was no way he could attempt to eliminate the merc as long as he had LeGault in such a compromising position. As much as Hornaday deserved his own fate, there was no justification for putting LeGault's life at further risk.

It was a standoff.

Until Hornaday made his move.

Bolan let the Beretta remain at his side, finger against the trigger. The presence of the 93-R didn't appear to concern Hornaday. He knew it was there and he must have accepted that whatever else Bolan might concede he would refuse to give up his weapon. The merc knew he had the edge, and he was going to play his hand right to the end.

For the Executioner the moment seemed to stretch. He had cornered Hornaday only to come up against a seemingly no-win situation. His mind raced wildly, seeking a way out of the standoff. Always at the forefront was Jack LeGault, the pawn in Hornaday's dangerous game. As long as he remained, there wasn't much Bolan could do. He could not—he would not—play with the man's life.

Hornaday held the cards.

It was up to him to decide which way they were dealt.

What Bolan had failed to anticipate was the introduction of a wild card.

In the form of Sanderson.

The Bahamian cop, despite his severe wounds, had made his way into the house and up the stairs.

He appeared without warning in the doorway, bloody and in a great deal of pain.

But there was still that rage inside him, boiling over now into righteous anger as he stumbled through the door, his handgun rising, aimed at Hornaday.

"Dead to fucking rights," he yelled, and pulled the trigger.

The bullet splintered the window frame inches from Hornaday's head. The merc jerked sideways, pulling LeGault with him.

The Magnum swung away from the DEA man as Hornaday picked up on Sanderson. He was forced into responding because the Bahamian cop wasn't following the rules of the game he had set up.

Sanderson fired a second time, the slug creasing the top of LeGault's shoulder. The DEA man twisted against Hornaday's stranglehold, still unable to break free.

The merc triggered the Magnum. The powerful .357 bullet took Sanderson in the chest, slamming him back against the wall. The second round drilled into the sergeant's skull. The force of the impact spun him, his weight falling against Bolan as the Executioner turned to go to his aid. Bolan tried to brace himself against the dying cop, feeling Sanderson's clawing hands reaching out for help.

Seeing his opportunity, Hornaday brought the .357 to bear on Bolan. His finger began to ease back on the Magnum's trigger.

LeGault made a final attempt to break Hornaday's grip. He partially succeeded and used his freedom of movement to drive his elbow into his captor's ribs.

The merc squeezed the trigger a fraction of a moment too soon. The bullet punched into the wall inches from Bolan.

As Sanderson slithered helplessly to the floor, his fingers closed around the Executioner's right hand, locking on to the Beretta. The unexpected weight dragged the weapon from the warrior's hand, leaving him defenceless.

Hornaday, cursing his missed shot, realigned the Magnum.

Still refusing to submit to the merc's threat, LeGault pushed his body back against Hornaday's, driving him into the wall.

With a yell of frustration Hornaday raised the Magnum, then slammed it across the back of LeGault's skull. The DEA man staggered beneath the impact. The merc lifted the gun a second time, intending to strike again.

In the seconds between the two blows Bolan, deciding on a course of action, left the Beretta still clutched in Sanderson's fingers. He shoved himself forward, driving across the room, closing rapidly on Hornaday. His eyes were fixed on the blurred outline of the Magnum as it whipped down at LeGault's head.

The heavy barrel struck moments before Bolan reached the merc. LeGault slumped forward, weakened by the blow. Hornaday loosened his arm from around the DEA man's throat as the man's body weight began to drag.

LeGault fell clear, and Hornaday began to bring the Magnum on target.

In that split second of time Bolan reached the merc. His right hand reached up to grab Hornaday's gun arm, forcing the weapon toward the ceiling. He heard the weapon fire, the sound distant. Then his momentum slammed him against Hornaday, pushing the man off balance. Locked together, the two men crashed into the window, the frame splintering, glass shattering.

Bodies twisting as they fell, Bolan and Hornaday tipped over the low windowsill and vanished from sight.

22

The sloping roof of the covered walkway on the far side of the house broke their fall. Tiles shattered, trailing after the two men as they rolled down the incline and over the edge. The drop to the ground was cushioned by a mass of thick vegetation, but the impact was still hard enough to leave them briefly helpless, each man struggling to draw breath.

Hornaday, realizing that he had lost his own weapon in the fall, climbed to his feet. He caught sight of Bolan, on hands and knees. A cold, unreasoning wildness welled up inside him. He launched himself at Bolan, kicking out. The toe of his shoe struck the Executioner in the chest, knocking him back. Hornaday, encouraged by his success, kicked out again.

Bolan, snapped back to reality by the force of the blow, saw the shoe driving at him again. He threw out his hands, grasped the shoe and twisted hard. The merc grunted against the surge of pain. He swung a wild punch that grazed the warrior's cheek, then followed with a backhand that split his lip.

The Executioner hunched his shoulders, pushed up off the ground and drove his body against Hornaday's. He slammed hard blows to the merc's ribs and felt the man back away.

For a brief moment the pair faced each other, seeking an opening. Hornaday struck first, a hard-driven punch that caught Bolan across the cheek, splitting the skin and spilling blood. Bolan let his head roll with the punch, then countered with a blow of his own that landed squarely over Hornaday's mouth. The merc stumbled away with blood pouring from his split lips.

He recovered quickly, advancing on Bolan, fists driving in at the Executioner. The merc was pushing hard, allowing nothing to deter him. He landed a couple of telling blows to his opponent's face and body, the wildness in his eyes coming through in the ferocity of his punches.

Bolan saw the desperation. He was facing a cornered man. Hornaday had progressively lost everything—his men, his base and even his final act of defiance. Now the man was going for his very life. If all else failed, Hornaday would strive to live.

Moving in low, the Executioner struck up at his adversary's body, landing a powerful blow over his heart. Hornaday grunted, falling back a step. Bolan kept up the onslaught, pushing in blow after blow, deliberately keeping up the pressure.

Hornaday stumbled over splintered remains of the shattered window frame. He slipped to one knee, and for a moment it seemed he might surrender. Then he broke into action again, snatching up a length of wood in both hands and lashing out at Bolan. The timber caught the Executioner across the side of the head, dazing him. Hornaday struck again, driving the timber down across the back of Bolan's shoulders. He fell to his knees.

The sound of running footsteps reached his ears.

As Bolan lurched to his feet, he caught sight of Hornaday vanishing around the side of the house.

He went after him, losing sight of the merc as he raced along the side of the house. He spotted him moments later, cutting across the front lawn.

Hornaday hit the street, veering to the far side as he spotted the bulky outline of a panel truck rolling to a stop. The truck, emblazoned with the logo of a local florist, had barely come to a halt when the merc reached it. He yanked open the driver's door and dragged the startled guy from his seat.

As Bolan crossed the street, he witnessed Hornaday's action. He heard the truck's engine race as the merc slammed his foot on the gas pedal. The vehicle lurched forward, tires smoking. The warrior raced across the street, coming up behind the truck. He made a desperate grab for the rear doors as the truck picked up speed. His fingers caught the handle, and he pulled himself onto the shallow rear step located below the doors.

Bolan was forced to grip the handle with both hands as the swaying motion of the truck threatened to shake him loose.

The truck tilted as Hornaday took a sharp right, tires squealing against the pavement. Bolan reached up with his left hand, hooking his fingers into the roof rack. He allowed his weight to be supported by his left arm, while his right hand tugged at the door handle, trying to free it. He felt it give. As the handle snapped back, the rear door swung open. Bolan kicked it wide, scrambling inside, and shoved aside the stacks of flowers and display baskets.

The cargo section of the truck was open to the driver's cab. Bolan was able to make out Hornaday's head and shoulders partly concealed by the driver's seat.

The open rear door banged against the side of the truck, attracting Hornaday's attention. He glanced in the rearview mirror, catching sight of Bolan as the Executioner moved along the truck floor.

Cursing, Hornaday began to swing the truck from side to side across the road.

Bolan was thrown off balance. He crashed against one side of the body, then the other.

A heavy impact threw the Executioner to the floor. The side of the truck bulged inward, and he realized that Hornaday had collided with another vehicle.

The merc's wild flight was starting to endanger others.

Gathering himself, Bolan covered the remaining distance in a headlong rush. He threw an arm over the driver's seat, closing it around Hornaday's throat. His left hand grasped the steering wheel, hauling the swaying truck back on line, away from the other traffic.

Hornaday freed a hand from the wheel, and rammed his clenched fist against the side of Bolan's head. As the warrior recovered from the blow, the merc hauled on the wheel, swinging the panel truck into a narrow side street between two buildings. Running free, the truck careered between the flanking walls, raising a trail of sparks as it dragged against the brickwork. The side mirror snapped off. The windshield's corner pillar buckled, and the windshield itself suddenly shattered. The cab was suddenly full of flying glass fragments. Hornaday caught the full impact, being so close to the front of the vehicle. Though he threw up his arms for protection, fragments got through, peppering his face with bloody gashes.

The truck bounced along for several feet, then jerked to a stop against one wall.

Bolan was thrown forward against the dashboard, pain flaring through his side as he felt a number of ribs crack under the impact.

With a grunt of triumph Hornaday hauled himself back onto his seat. He recalled something he'd seen on the floor of the cab and reached down to grasp it. As he straightened, he swung at Bolan, a steel jack handle in his fist.

The Executioner pulled back, conscious of the pain from his cracked ribs, and managed to avoid the handle. Hornaday struck again, this time connecting with Bolan's right shoulder. As the merc began to raise the handle for another strike, the warrior reached out, caught hold of his wrist and smashed it against the dashboard. Hornaday grunted, reaching out with his free hand to claw at Bolan's face.

A quick twist freed the handle, and Bolan used it against Hornaday, clouting him across the side of the head. Then, before the merc could protect himself, Bolan turned the steel bar and thrust it into his opponent's exposed throat. He put everything he had into the blow. He felt brief resistance, then the bar pierced Hornaday's flesh.

A hacking cough erupted from the man's mouth, accompanied by a pink froth. Bolan pushed harder, feeling Hornaday's body shudder violently beneath him. The merc slithered loosely from the seat to become wedged against the seat and floorboards.

Bolan slumped into the opposite seat. An overwhelming weariness overtook him. There wasn't an inch of his body free from hurt.

Somewhere in the distance he heard the frantic shrill of police sirens. They were moving in Bolan's direction.

The relentless pace of the past few days caught up with Bolan. He felt his energy drain away, leaving him totally weary.

He rested his head against the back of the seat and was still there when the first Bahamian cop stuck his head and the barrel of a gun through the truck's window.

"Stay right where you are," the cop demanded, then wondered why the battered, bloody American gave a low chuckle at his words.

For now, Medellín had been stopped in its attempt to add Jamaica as a base of operation in its ever-expanding drug network. But Mack Bolan was a realist, knowing that it was only a matter of time before the cartel would make another foray into the islands.

And the Executioner would be waiting.